Learning the Mother Tongue

Washington County Public Library
Oak Hill and Valley Streets
Abingdon, VA 24210

A Breakthrough Book
No. 53

Learning the Mother Tongue

Stories by Cathryn Hankla

Cathy Hankla

13 April, 1989

University of Missouri Press
Columbia, 1987

Hankla, Cathryn, 1958–
Learning the mother tongue.

(A Breakthrough book; no. 53)
Contents: Fishing – The moped massacre – The baby, the parrot – Learning the mother tongue – [etc.]
I. Title. II. Series.
PS3558.A4689L4   1987   813'.54   86-16123
ISBN 0-8262-0622-0 (alk. paper)

∞™ This paper meets the minimum requirements of the American National Standard for Permanence of Paper for Printed Library Materials, Z39.48, 1984.

The author gratefully acknowledges the following journals and their editors for first publishing some of these stories: "Fishing," *Artemis*; "The Baby, the Parrot," *The Chattahoochee Review*; "In Search of Literary Heroes," *The Texas Review*; "If it were Dark," *Fiction/86*.

Many thanks to The Snack Bar Poets for their friendship.

This book was brought to publication with the assistance of a grant from the National Endowment for the Arts.

For Mother and Daddy

Contents

"Such things as these are the mother tongue of our imagination, the language that is laden with all the subtle inextricable associations the fleeting hours of our childhood left behind them."

—George Eliot

"Beyond this there is nothing but prodigies and fictions, the only inhabitants are the poets and inventors of fables; there is no credit, or certainty any farther."

—Plutarch

Fishing

One time Kirt and I went fishing. He is my uncle. It was on a hot Sunday afternoon, and I got this idea in my head that I had to go fishing. Momma and Daddy were out playing golf. Grandmother and my two hundred aunts were all sitting in the back yard in green metal chairs under a huge oak tree. It was shady under the tree. I could not stand it under there, because it felt like fall instead of summer. It was August, and I wanted to go fishing.

Kirt said, "All right, we'll go." Then he went under the oak to tell the others while I stood in the sun. They were all against it. It was Sunday and, therefore, it would be improper. I was crushed, but I mumbled, "All right, it doesn't matter." But Kirt knew how I really felt. He pulled me aside and whispered, "We'll go anyway," and laughed. He left me standing in the shiny overgrown grass and ducked into the basement from the outside entrance.

I was fishing and catching the big ones. Long, glistening, pink trout. It was a wonder. It was magic. Everyone had come along to watch and listen and chuckle. I performed feats of strength and daring, extracting the shiny fins from clear, white water. I began fly-fishing and whipped the line in and out of the water. Sometimes it barely touched the surface. Backward flung, my hook caught fast, and I pulled with all I had, toppling my milking stool. I sprawled face down on the ground beside a thick, ceramic pot. Its contents were spilled over me, burying me under soil and geranium.

Kirt said, "That was a big one, wasn't it?"

I said, "It was a whale."

I could not help crying.

Kirt helped me up and held me in his arms for a while.

When I came to, the bucket was gone and the stick and the string and the paper clip. I stayed under the tree for a little longer, sitting on the stool.

The next Sunday the chairs and the people were reset under the tree. Kirt and I went walking down into the yard until we could not hear their chatter anymore. He stopped and stooped down.

Kirt had spied something under a holly bush. He called to it by name, "Hello, Mr. Tortoise," and held out his hand to it.

"What is it?"

"It's a big snapper."

"A what?"

The thing looked out from under the stickly bush and raised its wrinkled head. Its eyes popped and rolled. It was ugly and brown.

"Here's a stick."

"What for?"

"Turn him over, and he'll go away."

"I'm scared."

Dangling the stick in the turtle's direction, I jerked it back. I tried again. Every time I got the stick within inches of the brooding brown thing, Kirt would yell, and I would jerk back and shiver.

"Stop it!"

"What?"

"You know, stop it!"

I raised the stick, then slowly lowered it until it touched the bumps on the thing's shell.

"Go on, turn him!" Kirt urged.

"Shhhhhhhhhh!"

The stick touched his belly, I squatted for leverage and flipped him with one upward heave.

He rolled from side to side, then stopped. His feet churned the air. The air made circles. I gasped and buried my head in Kirt's white, stiff shirt.

"You said it would disappear," I whined.

"No, I said he would go away."

"Turn it back, turn it back."

Kirt reached down and picked the thrashing thing up in his large, hard hands. He petted it and laid it back down, right side up in its damp, shady home under the holly bush. It wandered away until I could no longer see it.

"I didn't want to make you cry, Sweetheart," he said.

Later that day we went to look for the turtle. It had disappeared. We looked under the holly bush and the prickly leaves scratched my back, but we could not find the turtle anywhere. I asked Kirt where it was, and he said, "It's Sunday, and all the turtles have gone to the evening service."

"Really?" I asked.

"Yes," he replied, and confidentially added, "Turtles always go to church."

It never occurred to me to wonder why it had been out wandering around earlier that day, so I did not ask. Maybe it had been out for a stroll between church times, too.

Later I asked one of my aunts about it, and she answered, "Turtles certainly do not attend church."

The next Sunday we went back home. School was ready to start, and I had to go to first grade. Momma and Daddy talked all the way home. I hung my head out the window and spit into the rushing air, squinting my eyes. I held out my hand, cupped, and let the air ripple like a fish through my hand.

"Get your head back in this car before I spank you," Daddy said.

"Comb your hair, it's a mess, and we're almost there," Momma said.

I stuck my tongue out at her, but she did not see it. We stopped at my other grandmother's on the way home. I pretended to be tired. Momma dragged me from the back seat and made me go into the yellow house. It was dark inside and real hot.

Fishing   3

"Talk to your grandmother," Momma said.

"Straighten up," Daddy said.

"She's tired and cross," Momma told my grandparents.

"Wave goodbye," Daddy said.

I slept all the way home.

Every morning at 7:30 I walked to the bus stop all by myself. I was the only first grader on my street who got to do that. I was proud.

School was boring. I had gone to kindergarten for two years before and knew it all. I got spankings every day for stuff I knew not to do. But I could not help it—first graders are so dumb.

One Saturday morning I was rocking in my chair sucking on a piece of ice. I still had my pajamas on because they had feet in them and were warm. The elephant cloth creased around my ankles but never scratched. The magic drawing board was making a pirate on "Captain Kangaroo." I was impatient for Mr. Greenjeans to come on with the animals when I faintly heard the telephone ring. Mr. Greenjeans came carrying an aquarium under his arm. It had tiny pink fish swimming in it.

As I climbed the stairs to Momma's room I heard footsteps and sobs. Peeping around the corner, I saw Momma crying.

"What's wrong?"

"Grandmother passed away," she said softly.

Just then my sister came into the room and said, "You don't understand, you never knew her." She was talking to me.

"Yes, I did, she was sitting under the oak tree the day me and Kirt went fishing, yes, I did know her, Momma, tell her I did!"

But I did not understand.

"Momma, are you going to make reindeer cookies for me?"

"I don't think so; not this year, dear."

"But you promised," I said. "You promised."

On the morning of Christmas Eve it started snowing.

Cathryn Hankla

Great round lumps of wet snow fell and covered up the car early in the morning before we got up. Church was canceled.

"Come on, we're ready to go," Momma called up the stairs.

We started out in the thick snow. It was uncrushed on the road when we left. Our headlights were the only ones on the road. Daddy steered the little car like a sleigh with a horse, I thought. We had to be there before 2:00. A snow plow passed us on the wrong side of the narrow, curving road and pushed us across the highway. We dangled over a bank twelve feet high.

Momma was crying. I did not know why. "Don't move, children," she said. We edged out of the car and sat on the back of it while Daddy and two whiskered men tugged the car out and cleaned off the snow-sprayed windows.

The house was quiet, and every time I said something, someone told me to hush. I was mad by the time I heard the cars pulling up in the driveway below. In stocking feet I scooted across the wooden floor of the hall to look out the window. I stopped and winced. A long splinter had hooked my foot. I hobbled over to the bed by the window and buried my head in Grandmother's pillow.

Daddy finally came home and pulled the splinter out. It was an inch long. I lost it on the rug after he gave it to me.

Before we left, they folded up Grandmother's bed and put it in the guest room. I was out under the oak making a snowman when Momma called me to go home.

The Moped Massacre

It starts with Johnny studying his palm, maybe looking for a way out of this one. He's lost in the interface, the space between his headline and his heartline. The wider the avenue the more logic will prevail. His lifeline zooms down, a chain-link fence around his thumb. Sever the thumb, he thinks. Sometimes he feels like taking his Swiss Army knife and tracing that line until his thumb hangs free or falls off into his lap. When he's not chain-smoking he thinks like that, and sometimes when he is. Like now, when with a cigarette dangling out of his mouth, he contemplates his fate. The space between his head and heart lines narrows as he waits.

His face looks too young to be his face, streaked with red clay rivers he paws at when it's hot and sweat trickles down his forehead. The black leather jacket never comes off. His mother long since stopped yelling at him to wash behind his ears. She'd be happy, if she still had the energy, to see him wash in front of them once in a while. The only way she can stand him now is to act like he's not around, which is easy because for the most part he isn't. He's out on that bike of his which she wishes she'd never let him have. But she didn't believe he would actually mow lawns to get it. He could do the normal thing if he had to. For a summer he had taken the old mower and managed to make enough dough to buy the bike. He sees it as a stepping stone, an interlude machine that will lead him, in time, to greater things, to the bike he has been heading toward all his life, when he is old enough, a street bike that will take him out of

6

this neighborhood and into the real world. But lately he has stopped thinking seriously about the future.

He's got his knife out of his pocket where it has been pressing against his thigh. He thinks maybe it might be interesting to pull his pants down and look at the impression of the knife he knows is there. But instead he rubs his pants above the spot and looks around and sees no one and reaches into his jacket pocket to pull out the orange he's been carrying around since seven in the morning. Nothing to eat all day, and now the shadows are lengthening around him; his own shadow is skinny and strange. The knife splits the skin of the fruit easy as shaving the skin off the top of a callous, or as hard. He tries to pierce the skin and no farther into the orange. If the white membrane holding the fruit gets ripped open he's not happy. He'd rather not eat the orange if that happens, and since he's hungry now he's very careful, circumnavigating the sphere once and then again, crisscrossing the poles. Prying loose a corner he begins to remove the skin in quarters. It's going to break half way, so he quickly traces the sphere two more times between the first two boundaries. Now it peels easily and the membrane stays intact, ready to be opened into slices. The sound it makes coming into halves he knows by heart, wonders if anyone else hears these sounds well enough to memorize them as he does. Oh well. The first section of the orange feels like a tongue on his tongue before he crushes it and the juice billows out of his mouth like steam from an old chugging engine. His eyes dart up and down the street as he eats the orange section by section, peeling and eating, peeling the sections away from each other without looking down into his hands. There's money in his pocket but it never burns a hole there. He'd rather not eat than spend his allowance on food when he can eat at home for free. He can eat for free if he makes himself go home, that is. "So you see," he can hear his teacher saying, "there's no free lunch." When he heard that, he wondered whether his mother ever had to hear about economics in the ninth grade.

She probably heard it in college. Sometimes it all comes so fast at him that he feels as if his best years are over and done with even though he is only dangling over the edge of fourteen and looks twelve if the leather jacket is disregarded along with his blank expression. All he has to do to make Mary Beth practically cry is to smile in her direction. It makes him feel like a jerk every time he tests out this theory and finds it to be true.

"So what do ya wanta be when ya grow up?" his uncle asked him when he was five. He thought and thought, with his uncle staring down at him, and he tapped his Sunday shoe on the foyer slate. "A tapdancer?" His uncle smiled.

"No," Johnny finally answered, when the question had become a vivid picture in his mind. "I want to be a milkman."

"What say?"

"I want to be a milkman." He heard his uncle laughing, repeating to everyone in the kitchen, yelling it down the hall, "Hey, ya oughta hear what Johnny just said! He wants ta be a MILKMAN when he grows up!"

His uncle scooped him into his skinny arms, rubbing his mustache into his hair, and set him back down again. The picture inside Johnny's head tried to blurt out—a picture of horses and jingling milk bottles and a white suit and a big black-banded hat.

"Horses," Johnny said. "I want to have the horses."

"That's a cowboy's job, not a milkman's," his uncle said, with relief. "Now that a boy, that's a better thing to be. That's my boy." The man kept smiling.

Neither alternative was something that still existed. The image of the milkman had been a picture in a book. And the image of cowboys his uncle held originated in a John Ford film. Johnny's mother bought the milk at the supermarket, and the beef, too, already cut into appetizing pieces, wrapped in plastic, ready to heat and serve. No cattle drive was part of that. No self-respecting steer, now plastic wrapped, had ever beaten a dusty trail across the plains.

Cathryn Hankla

The orange is eaten. Diamonds of orange skin lie around the rims of his tires like freshly fallen leaves. He has an instinct to pick them up, not to be a litter bug, but remembers that they are part of the earth, that they'll disappear in time. So he pitches the peels into the yard instead. To drift down the hill he doesn't need the pedals. Gas gets to the engine and he's off, steering down the side of the street, passing parked cars and watching a child wave to him from a tricycle. He waves back but too far along, checks the side mirror to see the child, but the tricycle's gone. Slowing to a stop at the sign, he puts both feet on the street and waits a second even though he knows no car is coming. He's practicing for when he has a Harley and must obey all the rules of the road. Already, he knows them, has the rule book memorized, knows when to pass and how to keep the bike in the middle of the lane for safety, how to keep the headlight burning and the chin strap of his helmet snapped. Wind brushes his hair back as he turns right, headed for the woods and Mary Beth who will be waiting, drumming her chapped fingers on a fallen log, waiting for him and maybe doing her math.

"Johnny," Mike told him last week, "you're an idiot if you don't."

"Why don't you shut up?" Johnny said and made a step toward Mike.

"You know what I mean," Mike said. "She practically begged you for it. I should be so lucky. You got an older woman who wants it and you haven't got the nerve to take it."

"You're stupid," Johnny said, sitting down on his bike and looking off down the street. He reached into his pocket and slipped on his sunglasses.

"So what? So what's that supposed to mean?" Mike curled up his lip.

"End of discussion."

"What? You're weird, man. All I'm telling you is to get it where and while you can. Mary Beth's got tits, you know. It's not like she's ugly or something. Does she have her license yet?"

"Will you shut up about Mary Beth. You don't know anything about it." Johnny's glasses reflected the road.

"I know more than you do. You know Angela? I know what kind of bra she wears."

"Big deal."

"It is a big deal—it's more than you know about Mary Beth."

"She doesn't wear one."

"What?" asked Mike, taking his hands out of his pants to make a fist for emphasis. "So you have done something. I thought so, I thought so. Boy, you had me worried there for a minute." Mike punched playfully at Johnny's arm, then asked, "What'd you do? Did you get to third?"

"Will you talk English? First, second, third, fourth. Big deal." Johnny zipped up his jacket, ready to go.

"Hey, wait a minute, we had an agreement," Mike said.

"That's kid stuff, Mike. Go and talk to David if you want to know something that's somebody else's business. I've got to go. See you later." Johnny was off, leaving Mike on the curb in front of his house.

Mary Beth twists her hair, looking up the answers in the back of her algebra book; she's already done all ten problems. Numbers one through five are right, number six is wrong, number seven is right, eight is right, too, now Johnny finally bends back the branches with his jacket sleeves and comes toward the log silent as an Indian. Mary Beth looks up, shuts the book, waits for him to sit down beside her on the log. She doesn't say he's late, just looks at him, pushes the hair out of her face.

"I'm late," Johnny says and sits down, turning toward her as best he can.

"I got all my problems done. One's wrong, though." She sets the paper, pencil, and book next to her feet.

"How long can you stay?" he asks.

"Oh, a while, it doesn't matter, as long as I get back for supper."

"Did you miss me?" he asks.

"Sure," she whispers.

He takes her hand and pulls her closer, as if to say that he missed her too. He can ask the questions but he can't answer them. So far it doesn't bother Mary Beth. Johnny puts his arm around her and closes his eyes before he moves his head toward hers; his lips, on target, touch hers; they let their mouths sit against each other for thirty seconds or so before they open and really kiss. It's maybe not so bad that she's in senior high and he's finishing up junior high when there's something like this to look forward to each afternoon.

Sometimes she acts as if she cannot stand it much longer with his tongue inside her mouth pressing against her tongue and feeling so big and crazy, like an animal trying to bore its way into the ground. Her breath comes slowly, and when he releases her she has to gasp the oxygen in a few times to make up for her loss. It's funny, though, he thinks, how soon she pulls him toward her for another kiss, even if it scares her. He does, then stops.

"Why don't you put your tongue in my mouth?" he asks.

"I don't know. Maybe because you have yours in mine?" she says.

"Okay," he says, and kisses her, opening his mouth, waiting for her to press her tongue inside. When she doesn't he pulls away and looks at her. She laughs before he can get mad and he kisses her again; this time she uncurls her tongue and strains to put it in deeply. He sucks on her tongue as if to pull her deeper. It's as if she's being swallowed, so she slips her tongue back into her own mouth. But before she can take a good breath he presses his tongue into her, and she sucks it the way he's just taught her to. She likes the way it feels inside her stomach when she does it. And before they can think, they've fallen off the log and onto the leaves, and she can feel him hard against her leg while he kisses her and she holds his tongue inside as long as she can.

He stops and rolls beside her. "We'd better quit," he

says, sort of sadly.

"Why?" she asks, but she knows why, he thinks. Sometimes they get beyond this point and then she has to tell him to stop before it's too late. And it makes him mad, but she has to say it. She shouldn't argue with him now, because she'll just have to say no later, and it's easier to let him say it now than go on. In his eyes she sees her face, upside down, and it's impossible not to kiss him again and pull him on top of her. It feels so good, but the hardness against her thigh is as tight as the lump in her throat. We can't, they think. She puts her hand between him and her leg. He puts his hand on her breast in return.

She doesn't know what she's doing really, but she rubs his jeans until he looks at her funny and says, "I'm tied in a knot."

She reaches into his jeans and finds him coiled, straightens him and leaves the ridge in line with his zipper, just beneath his belt. He closes his eyes while she does this and when he opens them he seems amused, but serious, too, and stays on his back but reaches over and begins to rub her crotch while he stares straight up into the sky.

It surprises Johnny that Mary Beth doesn't move his hand away. After a while she reaches over and runs her fingers up and down, tracing his zipper.

"Stop," he says, afraid that he's going to lose it any second.

She does, waits. He resumes rubbing her and then moves to unzip her slacks. She should stop him now, but she doesn't. She's not moving, he thinks, and wonders if he should go on. When she's unzipped he sees the elastic of her underpants and puts his index finger beneath it, moving his finger side to side along the seam. Once he climbed to the top of a steep cliff to dive into a lake and stood there for a long time. The longer he stood, looking down into the green water, the more rocks he thought he saw just beneath the surface. But at last he dove in and heard the shouts of his friends vanish as the water rushed around his head and body after the plunge. It was shallower than he thought and his hands slapped against the bottom of the lake before he turned and surfaced.

While Johnny tugs down his jeans Mary Beth waits. She doesn't make a move forward or backward. Why he is exposing himself he doesn't know; he still expects her to stop and go home. His erection stands straight out, like a soldier, as soon as he gets off his underwear. She's looking at it and at him, as if she's making up her mind for the last time. He peels her slacks down, then unzips his jacket and places it beneath her before he pulls her underpants off and finds his way, slowly, inside her. There's hardly any friction, she's so wet. It is as if they've always been lovers; and they don't know enough to know it isn't always so easy, like this.

When Johnny comes he jerks back out of her in a hurry as if he can pull the river of possibility backward with his prick. It seems as if, after the fact, he's known all day exactly what would happen. He's tried to delay the inevitable by making himself late for their rendezvous. It didn't make a dent in fate, he thinks. She asks for his handkerchief and he watches her wipe between her legs. A little pool sits on his jacket lining and when she sees it she wipes at it, leaving a damp spot. It's time for her to leave. They're not saying anything as she reaches for her pants. He wants to stop her, keep the together-time going. How can we just go home and eat supper? It's impossible, we're not the same. Stay. He kisses her and forces her back onto the jacket. At first she resists and then reaches for him, guides him inside her. It's the first time in his life he's done one thing without thinking of another.

"I'd better take you home," Johnny says. "You're late."

"I'd better walk," she says and shivers with the cold she's begun to notice.

"Come on," he insists, "I'll let you off at the corner."

They'll see us, her look says. But she follows him out to the road.

The Moped Massacre   13

"I can't believe it," Johnny says, once they're at the end of the path. Mary Beth pops out from behind him, stands at his side looking at him, wondering what he means. "It's gone," he says and turns to her.

"Are you sure?" she says, and he wonders why she's saying it.

"It was against the curb, right here where I'm standing and now it's gone. Somebody's got my bike."

"Let's look for it," she says.

He stands with his hands pushed into his pockets, as if Mary Beth has just told him to get lost. Finally, he answers, "You've got to get home."

"I'll go home and then I'll come back and find you and help you look."

"Thanks, but I don't think we're going to find it. Somebody's taken it. Come on, I'll walk you part way home."

They could talk if they wanted to, the walk is slow, but she just holds onto his hand and he can't think of anything except the blank place against the curb where his bike used to be. A block from her house they stop. Mary Beth tilts her head back, expecting a kiss.

"It's really cold," he says, wondering at how calm he sounds.

"Yeah, it might even snow. I hope you find it," she says.

"Thanks," he says, but doesn't try to kiss her good-bye.

Johnny watches Mary Beth walk toward her house, watches as she weaves across the sidewalk. He wonders if she knows he's watching, whether she'll ever turn around. He's never felt so mixed up, so shy and bold. Half of him floats inside, not caring about anything but her and what happened to them beside the log, half of him in shock about the missing bike, filing through faces in his mind, trying to see who it could have been, asking himself if he knows anyone that mean.

He's got to walk home in the dusk alone. Before turning the corner toward his side of town, away from Mary

Beth's, he decides not to tell his mother that the bike is missing. If she notices anything it'll be a miracle anyway. Digging in his pockets he finds matches and cigarettes. When he brings one to his lips he laughs because the cigarette is crushed. Between his fingers it breaks open like the neck of a straw-filled bear. He lifts another and manages to get it lit, then stuffs his hands back inside his pockets, cigarette on one side of his mouth, blowing smoke out around it when he must. It's been a long time since he's had to walk anywhere.

Right after supper he makes some excuse about homework and heads into his room. His mother's eyebrows go up, but she doesn't say anything. He knows what she's thinking, what she always thinks: that if his father were around, things would be different—that if Johnny had a father's influence he'd turn out better. Why she thinks this is anyone's guess; Johnny thinks she's blaming the present on his father for some reason that has to do with the past. Sometimes it seems she'd rather he had never been born, but that's not a thought Johnny can handle for long. It's easier just to try not to think about her at all.

Hours later, she calls good-night from her room to his. She's used to hearing no answer. Johnny's sleeping, already in dreams half repeating the events of the afternoon, half inventing them anew. There's something missing in the dream, always something awry: he kisses Mary Beth but when he looks her in the eye it's someone else; they ride away on a motorcycle and out into space; he enters her and never returns.

Sometime in early morning, with an intuition of snow that only children trust, Johnny rises from dreams and pulls his curtain back, gazes out into the circle given off by the streetlight and sees the white lumps falling, falling swiftly, steadily over the October leaves he's not yet raked. First snow.

"First snow's the prettiest," his mother said, as she bundled him into a snowsuit for an afternoon of sledding he would only remember through pictures in an album she would stop adding to when he turned ten. She snapped the seams and tied his mittens onto little metal loops at the ends of each sleeve so they could not be lost. He stamped into his brown rubber boots. Finishing the job with a stocking cap pulled over his eyebrows, she said, "Stay right there, while I get the camera."

She followed him outside, pulled his sled with one hand, holding tightly to the camera with the other. She had him sit on the sled while she snapped several pictures.

Johnny doesn't know how long he's been staring into the falling snow. The window frames divide the scene into quadrants that hold similar but different pictures. In the top left, from his angle, is the glowing lamp of the streetlight surrounded by swirling specks which might be insects taken alone. In the top right the roof of a house juts out from the darkness, recedes into dark that the eye can't follow. Bottom left and right connect a rusted swingset rimmed in white to a solitary oak catching snow in the part of its leaves it still holds aloft. Johnny looks from swingset to tree, isolating each framed picture: the swingset he lifted out of its concrete by kicking too high; the tree he used to hide in when he couldn't face his mother with guilty eyes. He remembers the time he bounced a golf ball off the driveway to watch it come back onto the hood of her car with a smack. Maybe that was what turned her against him. He wonders how it is that decisions made in an instant should be irrevocable. Why isn't an apology ever enough to turn back time, to erase the thing that has happened and continues, through memory, to replay through the minutes adding into a string of years? Some time ago his mother spent a few minutes without thinking what might happen afterward—early minutes when, not knowing who she was, she was unafraid to act, to share what she would later fear in herself, what she would try to hide from. None of this sweeps through Johnny in words, but it is a mood that chills his hands on the windowsill, while he cannot take his eyes away from the snow as it covers everything he knows and loves.

He moves to pull a blanket up around his shoulders,

and when he does something flashes into his eyes that he hasn't noticed before. Perhaps he's been too attentive to see it, but there it is, a flash of chrome just at the edge of the circle of light. In a few seconds he's pulled on his clothes, slipped into his boots and jacket, failed in finding gloves or hat, and stolen down the hall to the front door missing every cracking place in the floor. At times like this he's glad his mother never let him have a dog.

As his hair catches the snowflakes, making him white-headed and strangely old, he tracks toward the piece of chrome, knowing what it is but still hoping that it isn't what he most fears to find. Several inches of snow spread over the yard and half-assed stacks of leaves he's kicked off the sidewalk into bunches have made the landscape smooth in its unevenness. Familiar holes and hills have filled in so that he's never sure where he's stepping. It could be the dark, but he blames it on the snow. "Damn," he mutters, when his ankle twists down into a shallow furrow he's forgotten was there. He shakes his leg and the sharp pain settles. As he nears the shining thing he sees what it is: the handlebars of a bike sticking half way out of the ground, quickly disappearing from the surface as the snow deepens. He puts his hand on the grip jutting into the air and is certain. It fits his fingers, cold against cold. He snaps the piece from the ground as if it is the sword so long enshrined in granite, waiting for the one whose strength would be equal to the magic. He tramps the circumference of the yard to find a pedal, then another, a bit of bumper, a bent wheel, collecting the pieces as if they are scalps or parts of a dream he's trying to remember. Except for the cold turning his hands red and white, he might think it is a dream, and instead of struggling to carry all the parts at once he'd be struggling to wake up. Someone has ripped into his dreaming, severed his way of living and retreating, his way of traveling where he wishes to go, his way of leaving it all behind. It washes over him, the idea that someone could know him so well, and reach for the heart of the matter, and shatter it so skillfully.

The last thing he finds, flung into a high branch, is the chain. To get it down he has to climb up into the tree, leaving all the other pieces in a stack beside the trunk. His hands are so numb and tight that the first scrape of bark against them opens a wound he can't even feel. With the palm of his hand bloody he wipes some water from his face leaving a streak of war paint. The closer he climbs to the loop of chain the more he thinks he can never reach it, and his eyes play tricks on him, seeming to send the object farther and farther away, like the carrot the rabbit can never, point by point, quite reach.

To lunge toward the dangling chain would be easy. To push off into space, scarring the bark of the tree with his heels as he kicks free toward the chain, would be the thing he has been longing, without knowing it, to do. If he reaches the chain, grips it in his hand, there will still be parts which are missing. But when he kicks against the branch of the tree, briefly feeling the sting of his ankle, and spreads his arms out with the rhythm of a diver, he arcs toward an ancient desire without a care in the world.

Cathryn Hankla

The Baby, the Parrot

"Repeat after me," my mother seemed to be saying, looking intently into my week-old eyes, still blue from the underwater world I knew so well. I understood immediately. It was her own name she waited to hear me say. And when the time came that I should say anything at all, it was her name I chose to speak, remembering, I suppose, the way she had looked on that seventh day as her face loomed large as a meteorite just above my reach.

There are some things I should tell you about my birth itself, but first let me draw you a visual aid, a map of the place into which I was born.

Before that first real encounter, my birth, I had already surmised several oddities concerning the topography of my home place. The way my mother huffed and puffed, it must have been due to the steepness of the lay of the land. Whenever we moved we seemed to be moving either up or down. In fact, it was this motion which was most familiar to me since the instant of my conception. Not yet knowing the concept *mountain*, I surmised that my parents had chosen a vertical plane upon which to settle. From the shadows which continually crossed the belly of my mother and then my eyelids, there had to be trees out there also. Mountains, trees, such was the world into which I toppled in my own good time.

Where was I? My Birthday. I remember that the daffodils had just bloomed, because yellow will always remain my favorite color. The daffodils in groves; Easter came early; and it began to snow after I had failed to arrive on schedule. I was only two weeks late, someone said at the time, as late as the winter. And so they boiled the water when the water broke and I began to stroke my passage down (or was it up?) to air. It had been so long, I hardly knew what to do with the air, so thin and pale, I tried to do without it altogether but this soon proved impractical and I was forced to adapt to the crazed ways of the others (inasmuch as that was possible).

It was on my seventh birthday I chose to announce my voice. I was weary of the way everyone was constantly pointing to *table* or *clock* or *candle* or to an animal, saying the names of the objects with a question mark turning at the end of each word. It had been going on so long, you'd think the language was composed merely of questions. I'd heard all they'd said, and I remained unimpressed until my seventh birthday when it came time for the cake. I can see it now as my mother places it just in front of my place as she did at that moment, seven years to the moment since my birth. Suddenly, I felt as if I were playing that whirling game we liked to play in the backyard, my friends and I, turning around and around with our arms swinging out and out until we lost balance and sank to our knees and the landscape tilted up over the clouds, the clouds tilting over and over and over the land until the world was spun and we seemed to be at its center in a hug of suspended time. Well, it was a lamb cake that she placed there at my plate. She'd made it herself, iced it with frothy white sugar and sprinkled it all over with coconut, put half a maraschino cherry for its mouth and raisins for its eyes and a candied pineapple for a nose. The row of candles was burning quickly down and I had to make a wish. All at once it came to me, what I'd been waiting to repeat, and the words were rolling off my lips the second the candles were blown out, "Thank you Joyce, for the beautiful cake."

They'd been waiting for my speech so long they hardly knew it had happened. Joyce, my mother, began to serve the cake on little paper plates I had pointed to at the supermarket (they were plain yellow), and then it happened. As my first words reverberated inside their hearing they began to back away from the table. It was like that time, many years later, when I was playing a game of Blind Man's Bluff in the backyard and I was "it." Putting my whole heart into the game, I was picking up speed and all the kids began calling my name. I thought I must be getting very close to someone so I really tore into the sprint. When I awoke, having bounced back several yards after my collision with the oak trunk, all the voices were splitting the air along with the literal ring of stars above my bloody nose, but the children had left. There, in the center of our backyard, alone with the villainous tree, I began to hear what I thought might be my mother's voice calling me to supper, but I was unable to lift my head off the grass to answer. Then it hit me, a nut shell from out of the leaves, a chatter of titmice and a buzz of yellow jackets drawn to the smear of my face, I knew I would never be able to move again, that I was imprisoned in my own accident, in my own backyard until that time when the real stars came out and my mother came out back to lock the storage room for the night.

Helpless in my own tongue, I smiled at my family, but they continued to back away as if the words I had chosen to say had offended them or, worse, did not exist.

Since that earliest memory, of my mother's face bending down toward mine, I had listened to the prattle of the parrot from the porch of the house into which we would move at the end of my first year, the house referred to in the tale about the oak tree. Before I knew I would encounter the oak or fail to speak until my seventh birthday, in fact, before I knew anything except the face of my mother bending over me, I had heard the language of the parrot's repeated phrases.

I was never to be privileged enough to set eyes on that particular bird (or so I imagined), but wherever I went for as long as I stayed on the planet of mountains and trees, I heard, in idle moments when my mind was at ease, the voice of the parrot out of the past like an obstacle or a beacon mysteriously meant, perhaps, as a sign. If

I could just remember or discover what the parrot had been saying. One word kept coming back to me although I was certain it could not have been more than the name of the parrot's owner, "Bill, Bill, Bill," like a lament. My parrot could repeat nothing else.

When I was twenty-four and just graduated from the university in oceanography, I wandered into the pet store on the very day, coincidentally, that a shipment of parrots arrived. There were three of varying prices, different types, I guessed. But one of them looked familiar, though I can't tell you exactly why. It was the way it cocked its head to one side, the angle of its wing as if in salute as I entered the store. I walked over to it and said hello. It said hello. I said, "How have you been?" It answered, "How have *you* been?" I said, "After you." It said, "After *you*." So I said, "Much the same, how about you?" "Much the same," it said. And I knew what I had to find out, so I didn't hesitate another second. "Bill?" I asked. "What happened to Bill?"

This is what the parrot said:

"Do you remember that Saturday you were up in the woods behind the town water tanks digging holes with a shovel in the clay?" I nodded and the parrot continued. "You dug out a kind of boat in the ground, you were trying to emulate the Indians of the pueblo, although you didn't know it, didn't even remember the book in which you'd seen the Indian dwellings in the cliffs. The little foot holes straight up the sides of the adobe had impressed you, so there you were digging with your mother's implement, a brand new shovel so shiny the sun shot off it bent like a spear into your eyes. You'd dug all afternoon and the sun was turning red; grit stung in the corners of your eyes so you had to blink more each second than the last. It was then that you found it, remember?" I couldn't remember so the parrot went on. "It was an arrowhead. You recognized it at once and scooped it into the palm of your hand. It was one of the several things you'd always hoped to uncover, like a four-leaf clover, a shark's tooth at the beach, or a penny flattened on the tracks below your house. In a fist, your hand fit around it better than the dirt from which it had been scraped. You kept it in the center of your hand while you balanced the handle of the shovel and continued to dig in that same spot. Greedy, you wanted another sign. One had not been enough. But you never found another. Not until many years later. That day you found the arrowhead in the grave you'd hollowed out, you dragged back home as the sun was turning to dusk, late for your supper. And when you opened your fist, your palm swollen and sweaty, your mother didn't recognize what it was you'd found. It wasn't any fun to have to tell her, so you simply washed your hands and ate the macaroni."

My lips fell flaccid; astounded, I wondered what else this parrot knew. He knew more than I did about myself; he knew things I'd forgotten, things I'd never remembered; in short, he seemed to have retained it all, though we'd never before talked, we'd never met, it seemed, or parted.

"China," I mustered energy enough to utter. I was digging for that which they had said I'd finally find. China; the other side. "That was it."

The parrot laughed in his fashion, "It was the past you found, the arrowhead relic."

"Do you recall," I had to test the parrot on his own turf, "I used to juggle in the backyard beneath the oak?"

"Yes, of course, the oak you ran into when you were 'it.'"

The parrot's mind amazed me once again. How had he known about the accident? I tried to remain calm as I continued my interrogation about juggling. "One day as I juggled in my usual way, crisscrossing the three apples back and forth, a fourth red apple appeared in the toss. I'd never juggled more than three and it took a few tosses for me to figure out there was an extra object. Just as I was going to stop the rhythm, catch up the apples and count them to be sure, the fourth apple sprang out of its arc and up into the air. I dropped the other three, trying to follow the path of the fourth's ascent through the branches of the oak. Apparently, it cruised through without hitting a single leaf, much less a branch, and into the sky itself. A dark dot rose at the pace of a helium balloon out of sight.

"About a week later I was juggling some oranges; an apple appeared in their midst. I hadn't seen it arrive, didn't know from which direction it had come. But all at once in the tosses of oranges, an apple. Right off I suspected it to be the same one that had sailed away. Again, I attempted to cease my juggling to examine the objects in and out of my hands more closely. Before I could catch all four fruits, the apple rose out of reach, into the labyrinth of branches above my spot in the shade. I ran out from under the tree to trace the flight of the apple, but all I could see was the sun, a million spheres of painful luminosity intercepting my vision of the escaped fruit."

"That all?" the parrot asked after a pause.

"Yes," I replied. "What do you make of it?"

"Nothing at all," replied the parrot.

Triumphant, yet a little disappointed that the parrot had failed so quickly, I shuffled my feet as if to imply that I was ready to leave the store and get on with my day.

"So," the parrot said abruptly, "you wonder what became of that apple, is that it?"

I perked up, "Yes, that's what I was wondering, if you don't mind saying, if you know, that is..."

"I'd rather tell you what happened to the three oranges."

I had forgotten, of course; how could I have let it slip my mind? When I ran out from under the tree to see the apple disappear a second time, I'd returned to find the oranges missing. It had alarmed me at the time, but I had simply picked up three small stones and continued to juggle while I wondered about the apple. The fate of the oranges. They'd slipped away like the notes of the clarinet practiced in the trailer park below our house. I never saw who played the instrument or the instrument itself. And the music made its invisible presence felt only for an instant. This parrot was smarter than I'd imagined. So I dropped the apples and the oranges altogether so he could get on with his story.

"Might I continue?" asked the parrot.

"Of course, of course, please do, forgive me," I muttered.

"Before I do," said the parrot, "would you do me the favor of looking in the palm of your hand?"

"But," I looked in my hand and saw—before I could say that my hand was not closed, therefore I was unable to open it—I saw the coin.

"Is it there?" asked the parrot.

"Yes!" I sang. "Yes, it's here!" I was so excited, I forgot to ask what it meant.

"To continue," the parrot began again, "I was reminding you about the arrowhead and the tunneling you did on the hill. That brings us back to origins. I suppose you might be wondering sometime in the future, if not at this moment, just where I derive from and what, if any, my connection might be with you. And then there's Bill about whom you originally asked. I'll be getting to that. But first, about origins. I was born in Bermuda and soon afterwards they netted me and gagged me and put me aboard a ship. We were packed two and three in a cage during the passage. Oh, it was terrible, but I will spare you the details. Let me just say that I was lucky to survive the trip and many I knew did not. I lived for several years with the first customer to see me in the shop that had ordered me from my homeland. It was in New York City that a man from Virginia, a pharmacist I believe, purchased me and took me back to his town to live. Eventually, *you* lived around the corner.

"I was already in my thirties before you arrived on the scene. But then the man, I guess I should tell you now, that the man whose name was, indeed, Bill or William, died, and his house was sold to a growing family, your family in fact. Is that right?"

I nodded. I was sure now that this parrot, whatever he might say, was telling the absolute truth.

"They had to get rid of me, I heard them talking. It seemed no one else in the family of the pharmacist knew or cared a thing about birds, much less parrots. I kept my mouth shut until one afternoon the pharmacist's daughter left the latch off the cage and I simply flew out to light in the top of the oak. I think they were actually relieved I had done it. You see, that way they were off the hook. I watched them move everything out of the house and drive it all away. Then I watched you move in. You had a habit of pointing up into the trees. I had to be careful lest someone follow your finger sometime and see me big as life, sitting in the top of the oak. I don't think even you ever saw me, though. Am I boring you?" asked the parrot.

"No, no, of course not," I said.

"I've ended up here," said the parrot, "as have yourself, and that's about all of it, I guess, except..."

"Except for the reason," I interrupted. "Why have we met here, now? Why have our lives intertwined in this way?"

"That," sighed the parrot, "even I cannot say."

I asked the owner of the shop how much the parrot was. When he told me, my heart sank. Thinking fast about how I could scrape up the cash, I thanked the owner and told the parrot I'd be back. I got in my car knowing there was something I had to do before I bought the parrot and took him home. I had to return to the town where we both had lived, to the town where I'd been born listening to the words of the parrot before any other sounds.

I drove obsessed with the journey. My mind went blank as the road ribboned on and on. I drove up mountains, around them, and down. I drove with my own demons, and angels flickered in the fields like fireflies. Every time the road veered left and curved quick as a whip snap, it left me weak from the fear that I would fail to turn the wheel at the next turn, that I would twist myself around the steering column and railroad the car into the side of a cliff or off one into a ravine never to return home, never to find it.

When I pulled into town and parked on the street where I had lived, it was past midnight. I walked up the hill toward the water tanks, feeling each step magnetize the weight of the world until I pulled it along beneath the arch of each foot. Each foot raised with its step a weighty world. I trudged up, tracing myself back to the crest of the hill, thinking of what the parrot had said about origins. Only the word itself bellowed through my throat, escaping in an O of sound. I had to crack the circle, get to the center somehow. At the crest of the hill I saw the drainage tunnels glowing slick in the street light. The first one, I remembered, was the height of a standing child and it went on that way until curiosity made turning back impossible even well after the pipes had narrowed and narrowed until you were crawling, then merely pulling yourself along by your hands and feet.

I had to enter the tunnels. The entrance was smaller than I remembered. I began humpbacked, heading into the darkness up ahead, trying to recall the way. I shut my eyes, the passage narrowed and began to rise uphill.

I felt myself recessing first into my own past and then further back, backwards to the heart of the world beyond the arrowhead. On my knees I struggled against the cold clay pipe to wedge myself against the slick floor. Then the passage made its final turn, whether left or right, I cannot say. I was stretched out in the pipe. It seemed to have been made on the mold of my body like a death mask, the fit was so perfect. Only my hands and my ankles could propel me through, up. It was a kind of crude swimming that I continued in until, until I did not know how long it might last. I had forgotten what I was moving toward, why I was moving at all, I only knew that I was going on.

I rested at an opening to the air, looking through the iron spokes barring me in, to the stars. It began to rain, the pings of water echoed as they touched the tunnel floor or hit one of the bars above my head. I crawled, swam on. The straight path climbed until it reached a place so narrow I could not go on. At the summit of my crawling I extended my arm into the space beyond. I touched it.

The ring was there. I could feel it although I could not see. I checked for the tiny stone. It was there. The ring fit, a little loosely still. As far as I could reach, into the last tunnel where the ring had come from, I placed the coin. It was after this that I remember hearing the water grow louder.

Escalating into a roar, the water noises came echoing from the source of the tunnel out to where I was wedged. Unable to turn around I began to push myself backward with my fingertips, arching my feet so they wouldn't slow the descent. The water first was present as a small trickle beneath my stomach. Instantly, it soaked my shirt. I raised my chin as best I could to breathe the musty, but necessary, air. Just as I had come back to the place from which I could look out and see the sky, I raised my head but the clouds had replaced the stars with rain. The water soaked my scalp and worked its way into my breathing until I gasped and continued on, backward, through the tunnel toward its opening in the street.

I hadn't gotten very much farther when the water came like an explosion, barreling down the pipes. An instant I heard the rush on its way, the next I was underwater, being swept underwater but down to the end of the pipe.

As if a giant wave had washed me ashore I landed at the mouth of the water pipe with the rest of the sludge. A shaft of lamplight fell against my hand and I turned it up to see the agate glowing in the tarnished silver setting. I had it, I had found it. I heard the parrot whistle from a branch; I heard my mother calling me to supper; I heard the voices of the dawn bustling out of hiding into the first hour of light and song.

It wouldn't be long now. I could pawn the ring and claim the parrot as my own.

Learning the Mother Tongue

When I asked for an Easter rabbit, what I got was an orange-dyed chick. "The bunnies were sold out," Mother told me. "Consider yourself lucky to have received a chicken." I said I would consider that, and I did.

* * *

"I'm going out in the *lard* to play, Mother."
"The what?" she asked.
"The *lard*," I answered.
"You mean the yard?"
"Yes, the *lard*."
"I think we should go see Dr. Straightair, tomorrow."
"I'm not sick," I said, so we went.

* * *

"She doesn't have any physical sign of a problem. No ear, I mean hearing deficiency, she isn't, certainly not, tongue-tied by any means, so I can't clip her tongue, no sir, that's not the problem."
"What *is* the problem?" Mother asked.
"A stubborn one, at any rate, consider this: 95% of the time they simply out-grow these things. You just wait until she goes to school, she'll be speaking correctly in two shakes of a rabbit's tail." Dr. Straightair winked at me.

* * *

"How's my little Dutch girl?" asked Daddy.
"Don't encourage her," said Mother.
"What's Dutch?" I asked.

29

"It means you talk funny," said Elsie.

"Do I talk Dutch, Daddy?"

"No, Chick, you talk real sweet," said Daddy.

*　　　*　　　*

"You just wait until you have to go to school! They'll make you change your name. You can't spell your name like that, with a 'C,' when you go to first grade!"

"Yes, I can," I said, not very certain.

"No, you can't," said the kid at the trailer court.

"Mother said so, she named me with a 'C.'"

"Things are different at school, you just wait and see."

"You're fibbing," I said, with faint hope.

"I'll bet you can't even count."

"One, two, three, four, five, six, seven, eight, nine, ten, eleven, twelve, *fourteen*, fourteen, fifteen..."

"*Thirteen*, fourteen, I told you you couldn't count, Stupid."

"That's what I said," I said, "*fourteen*, fourteen."

"And it's wrong! You said fourteen twice, you said it *twice*. Ha-ha, Baby can't count!"

"I can't say that one, but I know what it is."

"If you're so smart, say it."

I paused with my tongue against my top teeth.

"Chicken," he hissed.

"*Fourteen*," I said.

"I told you so!" said the kid at the trailer court, and he hopped through the arched door of his silver house.

*　　　*　　　*

"L-zee, there's a big worm in the entrance way," I announced.

"So what? I'm trying to read. Scram."

"You don't understand! It's BIG."

"Go tell Mother, she's digging in the backyard, in the flower bed."

"Mother?"

"Yes?"

"Mother, there's a *nake* in the entrance way," I muttered.

"A what?" asked Mother.

"A big worm."

"Whew, I thought, for a second, you said snake."

"That's it," I said, "A brownish head. It's gray with black blotches, and its tongue goes like this," I demonstrated, "in and out."

"A SNAKE, you said! In the house! Quick, get the rake! Geezus, sounds like a copperhead!"

"Copperhead," I said.

A Box for Dreams

Last night the fireworks flashed high over the water. Our beach was empty except for Mother and myself on the porch. We sat on the steps, held on to the wood, and saw the colors break. We listened. Mother pointed to the first explosion, so I would know where to keep watch. The huge arcs opened and spilled. Several times the fire burned clearly all the way to the surface of the water before going out. I could see the reflection of the light brighten, the closer the burning cinders came to the ocean. And at its peak of light, the two lights met. Both ended in that touch. Mother, after a time, circled my back with her arm, and I did not mind being close. The wind was cool last night. I could smell ozone. The ocean, calm, lapped rhythmically; I fell asleep, slumped against Mother's brown shoulder and arm. She nudged me awake and we went inside. All the noise had stopped overhead. All the lights were quenched in the sea.

When the sun came up they combed the beach searching for Daddy. Mother and I watched from the porch, watched the men wade and row close to shore in the surf. We watched their lights last night. And we watched long after they had left, looking out, hearing the crash of the storm.

In the blackness, the furious pound and echo. As if we were blind under the sky, afraid of the noise. The absent moon. Never to see, but only listen—the vast strength like breathing. The sound of something hidden, tossed. The pull—involuntary— toward something we strained to see.

*   *   *

Mother folds the shirts as she irons them, folds the sleeves toward the back after buttoning every other button on the front of each shirt, then she folds by uneven thirds, making a neat package. A stack is just beginning. All the shirts, so far, are blue. I sit on the floor making origami animals, scribbling now and then into my notebook.

"What're you writing?" Mother asks.

"A letter."

"To yourself?"

I stack seven squares of paper, white on one side and colored on the other. One yellow, two blue (navy and sky), one green, one orange, one pink, one crimson. Different sizes and crisp to touch. I have already folded a tiny purple fish, a brown chick, a black butterfly. What I wish I could make is a kabuto, or a boat. I pick the green square for the boat and begin folding back each corner toward the center, making ninety-degree angles of color against the white side. Then I fold the triangles under again on each of the four angles until there is a perfect square of white showing in the center. The top folds into the center to meet the bottom, and they split the white square evenly, hiding it. After this, the directions are not clear; the diagram turns cartoony and the boat is lost. I decide to try the kabuto, and begin folding the crimson sheet in half diagonally.

"What are you making now?" Mother folds a shirt.

"Nothing."

The corners of the triangle fold to touch the center point, fold back on themselves. There is a step between this and opening the center of the original diagonal to reveal the white of its insides that I cannot figure out, so I unfold the whole mess and start over.

Mother has stacked five blue shirts on the clean kitchen table and has begun another pile, placing a white shirt down first. The one she is ironing is plaid. While she folds, the iron moans and water beads on its rim and disappears into steam. Every shirt is perfectly creased to fit in the third dresser drawer below the T-shirt and underwear and sock drawer. The bottom two drawers are a mystery to me: maybe sweaters or handkerchiefs or bills. I do not know. Maybe they are empty or bottomless or stuck. I decide to try making a crimson frog. It looks easier than the kabuto. Only nine folds to a frog.

I make origami birds, string them into a mobile on a clothes hanger. Mother hooks it on the window latch. Rain on the beach, icy rain. The sheets beat the tin roof, and I think of the color of rust up there. We will have to paint it soon. Mother puts down the iron and starts a fire to cook our lunch. Here, we have a wood stove, although there is oil and electricity. We just like the wood stove. Daddy is still gone and there is still no news. I rock my chair with my back to the open blaze and rock the chair over, catching my hair in the flame, smelling the singe. Mother shuts the door of the stove.

"When will Daddy come home?" I ask. Remembering him I am younger, clumsy. I imagine I have caught my hair on fire, but it is way too short to have been burned, not loose enough to have caught a flame.

*   *   *

"I think it's between those lights in the darker part," Mother said, pointing. "We've been walking so long, it must be close. Why do you suppose they don't put lights on the footpath to the beach?"

"I don't know."

We kept up a steady pace to the spot between the lights.

"We're walking in the path of the moon," Mother said, looking down at the reflection we followed and distorted with our footprints. Lightning in the distance. It smelled like rain.

"Fireworks?" she asked.

"No," I told her. "It's going to rain."

"We'd better hurry, I'd hate to be out here in a storm."

Phosphorous focused on the water, the moon hazy; white foam blew off the sea; I can see it filling the air with iridescent bubbles when it flies into the path of the lights. She talks of the many lights, the "firedance" on the ocean, the feel of the sand, the sound that our feet make scooting across the little caps of its furrows. I think it sounds like a flying saucer. She laughs. We are almost to the path—she begins veering up the beach when something in the water catches my eye. Before the

next wave can wash in, I reach down and take it. Something
shiny, but my arm is too short; the light is an intermittent
current, not precise enough to identify the object. I want to
stretch, put my head underwater. Still, I could not touch it
with my feet on the sand, bent from the waist. To touch it,
I must pin my chin to my chest, strike fast as a fish, fast as
a diver breaks that barrier, fetch it and swim away from the
breakers without knowing what is inside my fist.

*　　　*　　　*

They are searching for a striped stocking cap, a gray
glove, a scrap of red flannel, a button embossed with
an anchor, or a green and brown rubber and leather
boot. Any one of these things could be the clue which
uncovers the man who is lost. It is the third day we have
stayed here without going out for anything. There might
be news, a knock at the wooden door, a hand scrubbing
the glass of a window that we would miss. So we stay.
But already my daddy has become *The Man Who Is Lost*.
We talk, my mother and I, about our dreams as if they
are all we know, as if they are evidence of our relation,
an excuse for sharing that makes his absence real.

"A green vista," she says, over the hiss of her iron on
his shirts. "Yellow foliage covers it entirely. The mountains
are beautiful, an eerie purple, misted with gray, but I
say to myself, in the dream, 'This must be paradise.'
When I say this, the heavens peel open with blinding
light, crackling thunder. Starch white horses fall out of
the clouds. Horses huge and pounding, they paw the sky,
split spaces into the cover of clouds; their hooves glint in
the daylight, shining white. It is terrible, then other things
float by: ice cream sundaes, banana splits topped with
maraschino cherries, misshapen clouds. People scurry to
purchase tickets for seats from which to watch all this.
They mumble, 'Miraculous, frightening, the first event in
years.' I watch through a window, amazed at the chaos
and color."

"I dreamed of a hot air balloon lifting off in the distance,"
I say in response to her dream, "its canvas the color of

a pale but vibrant yellow, the white-yellow of the moon seen through clean air. A long, green field flat all the way to the horizon where the gondola rises, slightly purple through the atmosphere, though it would be brown if I were near it. The sky is the color of a summer midday sun, or a sunset sun when the air is putrid, hot orange with a fiery pink halo."

"Do you remember catching your hair on fire?" Mother looks up from her work and asks. "You must have been about four or five. I had told you to go sit in the corner because you had let the cat in the house. You were rocking in the big rocker, touching your toes to the floor and kicking yourself backwards like you were on a swing. You rocked so hard the chair turned over; somehow you managed to land practically in the fireplace. I've never been so scared, I don't think."

"I remember," I say, not really remembering, but picturing the event the way she has described it.

"You've never liked your hair long since."

Is this the reason? I wonder.

*　　　*　　　*

We waited all afternoon. Mother read a thick novel. I looked at a book about Japanese packages Daddy had sent to Mother when he was in the navy. In the book were many boxes: compact, designed with rice paper symbols, made by hand. Paper boxes, reed boxes, strong boxes for jewels, boxes of wood, cloth, tapestry tied with rope. Boxes within boxes, and some made of leaves rolled tightly together, sealing, like grape leaves, something in their centers.

Boxes strung like mobiles are my favorite. Imagine them moving and spun, never spilling their contents. I guessed inside, but did not wish, ever, to unwrap one box after another for fear of emptiness—at the center there might be only broken shells. Where mother-of-pearl should slick the concave center, nothing but white, shaped in the smooth cup like something too new to look at or touch. And if I dared to touch that absence of color, to trace the lines of fingers, what would I discover? Something cool and rigid, sharp with the hardness and purity of a geode

. . . the secret boxes I closed my eyes to open. Even to imagine them open, my eyes must be sealed. I wished their contents to be feathers, down, sequins mixed up like many stars, or bits of stained glass from the windows of a church. I wanted to mold boxes myself, fill them with my own treasures. I thought what I might have to hide inside: colored pencils, little pink and white shells, five shell slivers bearing my initial that I had found on the beach all in one day, gull feathers, salty and dingy. I had a sand dollar big as my hand, and a pearl necklace from my grandmother in Roanoke. What kind of box could hold them all?

*   *   *

July 1, 1970

Daddy handed me this book, "For your birthday," he said. "I want you to have it, now."

In three days I will be twelve. Old, I think. Daddy always knows what to give me. I like surprises, like this diary, early, instead of on the right day. It's raining. Daddy's reading, smoking cigarettes, turning the pages with his eyebrows raised unpredictably up whenever he likes something. I hate his smoke, but I like to watch him read. This book is the best present. Yesterday, I was hiding and Daddy found me. I wasn't hiding, really. I wanted to think and look for shells. Sometimes, inside the caves, the most perfect shells wash up and stay. Nobody finds them, nobody goes there. It's better than the beach early in the morning for finding shells that aren't broken. When Daddy came home he showed me a spiral from a larger shell, the center part by itself. "This is the heart," Daddy said. I closed my fingers, balled the hand loose. I have a box I keep things in that I don't want to lose. This morning I dug the spiral out of my pocket in the dirty clothes and put it in the box without washing off the sand.

July 2, 1970

Daddy stood on his striped towel, straight, in orange

trunks and pointed up. "In the broad daylight, in all this sun," he said. I looked up. Kites cut the air; the plastic colors billowed, dipped in the sea breeze. Down the beach I saw the strangers reel them down. But Daddy was pointing at the moon. "Look," he took my hand. I shaded my eyes with my other hand; he didn't shade his eyes because he was wearing sunglasses. "It is the moon!" I said. I reached down for my bucket. Our three towels lined side by side were separated by thin strips of sand we'd run our hands in, sunning. Beside mine was the bucket with the giant silver spoon inside. I took them to the damp part of the beach where the water leaves a foam and pushed in the spoon. I liked the sound. I was careful not to bend the handle; it's an old spoon. I dug, filled the hole with water. I thought about starting a castle. Tomorrow, I will shovel more.

July 3, 1970

I'm bathing, writing propped in the tub. Daddy smokes on the porch, watching the waves break. His cigarette burns red. If I were on the porch I couldn't see his face clearly in quarter moonlight. Nothing but the small reflection of smoke against his face. I dab at my shoulders with the rough towel to keep them warm above water. I think he wants to buy a boat someday. During lunch he watched the sails and counted them aloud. I can see them as well as he can. I can count them for myself. But Daddy likes to count and say the colors of the sails. One boat, his favorite, has a purple and yellow sail. Daddy wears purple socks when he wears socks and yellow sleeveless tank shirts. He is a small man and blond. His arms are strong; he's quiet. I can make him laugh, and so can Mother. He's a fisherman. I've never smelled fish on him. Mother says someday he'll get better. I can't see anything wrong with him, though.

July 4, 1970

Daddy woke us. He shook me, lifted me up, carried me out the door to see the sun rise red on the water. All the time I was struggling to get down. Mother began to fix breakfast for him. He'd been up hours. In early light, in armor, the bathers slipped their bare skin into the gray ocean. Their suits keep them in, their shields and swords, their limbs and curious joints, creaking bones. One by one, they crouch in the ocean and bob. "It's sure to rain, go back to bed," Daddy said. "Sweet dreams, Birthday Girl."

*   *   *

An old dream

I went to their room; the door cracked open. Mother held his head, "It's a nightmare," she said. "Only a dream."

Daddy, on board ship, had been sleeping. Called up, groggy, told to bring a blanket, he crept to the top deck. The sea was breaking over the rails, and there was Mark, his good friend. Cold in the spray, Daddy shivered. Mark wrapped himself with the blanket, "Throw me over, quickly." Daddy did not move. "Throw me," Mark repeated. "I'm already dead." Daddy stood and saw him leap, saw the green wool blacken, the body sink down.

Mother woke me. "It's only a dream," she said and led me back through the dark hall to my bed.

This happened after Daddy gave me my first diary, but before he disappeared.

A new dream

Across the waves we go, I on her back, though I am nearly as long as she. Mother opens her hands, full of shells, all colors. They sift down beneath us—sift and settle. We swim beneath the cruelest water, land flat on the sand. The quick surf spins around us. Our heads rise, proud, hers in a bubbled cap and mine full of salt. I can't tell exactly how old we are. We snap up like turtles, rising on our arms, laughing, with our legs buried in the sand. Hard waves needle us, but we do not move out to ride in again. Instead, we lie, beaten, in sand. And the ocean moves around us. We are moved by it, but still. "We will sink to Japan," I say. But Mother does not hear, she does not blink or answer. I notice her hands, sunk to the wrists and sinking lower. I pull my own hands from their holes, making two murky pools. I start new holes. On my stomach, I watch her stare at the mounds of sand beneath which her hands are stretched, combing for something. The opening for her arms widens as she forces her fingers down; she wears the beach like bracelets, or handcuffs, the bones pulling the webs between each buried finger taut.

The Cartoonist

In the morning he woke with a blinding, a blatant headache. Through the chimney pealed twitters of impossible birds. Purple finches, he presumed, because these had been pointed out to him only the morning before by his wife, who was not here today. His name was Geb, and he sat in the chair in which he had awakened, listening to the echoing thrum; only wisps remained of a fire that had gone out sometime during the night. Beside the chair many cans were strewn, empty of beer. He had had no need to stack them neatly, neither had he felt the need to collect them into trash. They remained as they were, as it was, for decoration. From this dawn onward he pledged himself to litter, shrugged to leave his chair.

Failing this first maneuver of the morning soon to be afternoon—whatever time, it was his dawn—he slumped back down; his head sat upon his shoulders like a helium balloon unable to lunge, its gondola lined with recumbent stones.

It was safe to assume he would have to brew coffee by noon or face a hair-of-the-dog. Donald brought the newspaper, left it lumped at his master's feet and nearly barked. The paper had been thoroughly chewed of news, and anyway, Geb would notice soon that it was yesterday's.

He rose, he had to; rising, his head compounded. Geb opened the freezer compartment where his wife always stored the coffee beans, then plopped a handful into the grinder. The noise. "They're only two of us, you know. A pound of coffee costs..." An arm and a leg, Geb finished for his absent wife, and he smacked the air with his lips where usually she would be scooping grounds into the plastic filter top of Mr. Coffee with an accuracy he had never attained.

Geb found the day-old jelly doughnut and burned it to a crispy crunch in the toaster oven. Nothing else, so he scraped out the charred, berry center with his spoon, forfeiting the bottom, suffering third-degree burns, then the top because it crumbled, last the sides, enveloping the absent berry jam, because they made the clatter of rain upon a roof of red tin when they met the metal plate.

On the pink counter top he found what he had scrawled the evening before. A typewriter picture:

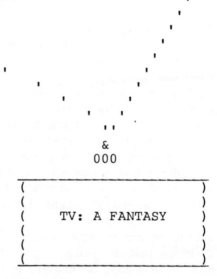

```
                                                    '
                                                 '
                                              '
                                           '
                                        '
         '                           '
                                  '
              '               '
                  '       '
                      '  '
                     ' '   .
                      & 
                     000
```

```
 ┌─────────────────────────────────┐
 (                                   )
 (                                   )
 (         TV: A FANTASY             )
 (                                   )
 (                                   )
 (                                   )
 └─────────────────────────────────┘
```

If serious you are, I'll be impulsively in jest;
If you be silly, I'll suffer wise and nearly serious.

Below it, he scanned what appeared to be a letter. When he ceased rereading it, he was still quite curious. He could not remember having written it:

Dear Friends,

Here in mute suffering we sit together (or nearly so—as so as close is ever together and sometimes farther, wiser, sharper in distance; you will remember all of it in solitude, so why remind you here and now together matters when apart is so often) in the crowd of individual fools, worthy and unworthy, we go among ourselves as guests. You remember it all in future tense. This'll be my gift, my legacy of chatter, sulking, and sincerely yours to take or leave, so here, together, sit we too, two and one and one, and one and two.

He hoped it had not offended his wife. Z. (short for Zippy, a name he had invented for her when he thought of her in private) probably had already left the house when this had been composed. He hoped so. In case, he took the piece of paper, crumbled it into a fist to affect the proper contrition. Maybe she had written it. Geb breathed a sigh, only halfway convinced. Anyway, he reasoned, it's possible that she (anything, indeed, is possible, isn't it?), it's completely possible that the message is harmless. Merely a bit of charged automatic writing. He relaxed and sipped more coffee, and his stomach gnawed.

Geb was making too much of it this morning, but his head smarted and that was all the smarts he could muster. "Use your kidneys!" his wife would have instructed, which was her way of saying, "brains." Thank you very much, he thought, not thinking very clearly or enough to be called succinctly. Donald chewed now on a moldy shoe, and he seemed to smother it in saliva, then slurp it off in growls. It made Geb's stomach churn; it also made him burp. He sat so quickly he sat on the kitchen floor and wondered what would become of him, because he was sure he would never get up.

It was here, in the kitchen floor's waxed center, that he remembered his dream of turnips. At the city market he liked to lounge against the brick shop fronts, licking his lips in the presence of so many and various turnips.

In fall, most people went there after last tomatoes or early pumpkins, or late, purple-ridged cabbages. They also went to buy berries, eggs, and flowers, apple butter and honey. But Geb went only and every Saturday morning to enjoy the endless sorts in row upon row of turnips. He trusted the purple/white ones to taste, but he also

The Cartoonist   43

bought the red ones and the solid whites to arrange in a fruit bowl. He had no use for fruits. Then he had tried to paint the bowl, a failure. Z. would cook them with carrots (leaving the turnips to Geb); she liked the contrast of colors, and the carrots. A success. When alone, he would boil only turnips together, mash them in a porcelain bowl with gobs of country butter and as much salt as he could bring himself to; a pinch of pepper on top he would replenish with each bite until the turnips were a memory in the white bowl. And all that was left might be a finger lick of butter speckled with freshly ground pepper.

Donald came and licked his face. Geb had always wanted a dalmatian, unlike Donald, who hid under beds when the fire siren blared. It split the air and Donald flew, howling. The cat, Baby Thing, was asleep on the counterpane in the guest room, and when Donald careened into the room, Baby Thing lifted a claw in case Donald decided to take the high ground. Panting, he took his place beneath the springs, however. Baby Thing put her foot into her mouth and began to wash it noisily.

Geb stood up, surfaced like an elephant, placing his left foot whole into the teeming water bowl, which had on it the word DOG, painted in large, block letters so that it could not be missed.

A starling eats "injurious insects, grains, wild and cultivated fruit." Its voice consists of "squeaks interspersed with pleasant musical sounds." Geb had read this in his *Vest Pocket Nature Guide to Birds*. Just then a starling startled him without sounding anything like music. All the birds at the feeder were fighting over suet. The blue jays thought it entirely theirs, so the starlings and the blue jays were agreed on this one point: they each owned it completely and would not give it up. The cardinals, the brilliant husband and the orangey wife, stared on annoyed because so much seed was being tossed across the ice. They could not condone waste.

The doorbell rang.

The doorbell rang twice.

Convinced his head would burst, convinced it was not bird song, Geb ambled to the door in good time, shaking his wet foot between steps.

"It's you, hello," he said, turning back into the kitchen.

"Hello," I said, and he grumped from the dimness, "Come in."

I scuttled off the iced entrance slate, into the foyer, carrying the morning edition of the *Times*, which contained Geb's comic strip, "B. Ird Starr." Geb was obviously in no mood to be anything other than oblivious that his Ird had moved onto the editorial page from its place of ten years, next to Billy Graham, next to Dear Abby/Ann.

I whisked into the cluttered kitchen, switched on the fluorescent light. Geb blinked, but he did not complain. I think he was glad I had finally come to egg him into the work at hand.

"Where's Clarice?" I asked.

"You should know."

Geb was right, I should have known, but I did not. And I did not ask again. I mustered a flustered expression.

"She's left until I finish the next two weeks," he said. "You can't get behind in this business. I've given her up for Lent."

"In the middle of the winter?"

"I got behind, and she threatened to visit her aunt if I didn't produce before yesterday, noon. She gave me until three p.m., then went out for a pack of cigarettes and hasn't returned. She left with a suitcase—how strange, I remember thinking, and she doesn't smoke, but I still believed she'd bring me the Lucky Strikes before she really left. She didn't."

"It wasn't my idea, I assure you."

"I wouldn't be too sure of that," he cocked his chin to the right.

"Why don't you pick up that idea you abandoned last month?" I tried to change the subject.

"That was yours," he chided.

It was true, but I had forgotten. I did not have the heart to show him where old Ird had been promoted, in the fix Geb was now encrusted.

"Have you tried your lucky penny toss?" I asked, tentative.

"No," came the quick reply like a slap.

"Have you, perhaps, juggled half an hour?" He shook his head.

"I Ching?" I tried again.

"Would you like a beer?" he interrupted.

"Last night I saw a doctor on TV who claimed that inversion was the very thing for every ill. 'This is no universal panacea,' he exclaimed. 'But I predict that soon infants will be ripped from the womb and hung upside down. It feeds the brain, heals many back complaints, abates the rat race, the paper chase, almost, some of my patients say, it replaces religion, or at any rate, it furnishes a peak experience.'"

"What do *you* think?" Geb inquired when I had to take a breath.

"You might try it." I raised my eyebrows.

He had a beer in his hand, but I did not think he'd actually open it. He tapped the tab as if checking to be sure it stayed snug. "You sure?" he asked me, indicating the beer. I nodded. He snapped the tab back and emptied the contents of the can into the sink. "The last one in the house," he explained, and I nodded my approval as the suds thudded the rubber lips of the garbage disposal, curled into the drain pipes, followed by a swirl of tepid tap water and a rush of spray erasing the scent.

"What are you doing here?" asked Geb.

"I brought your paper in; it blew onto my porch, I found it thus, this morning before eight o'clock. I waited until I felt quite certain you'd be up. Then I rang the doorbell three times and was about to leave your paper on the stoop, thinking you were not at home when you opened the door and admitted me," I explained.

"Clarice called and asked you to snoop on me, did she?"

I could not tell a lie. His question went unanswered, and he looked smug, superior, collected, all his ducks in a row. A dove cooed through the flue. And I thought the roof must be crusted with doves for a single voice to trumpet so loudly. I must have twitched with the gust of sound, because Geb smiled broad as a jersey and bit his tongue.

"Could I borrow a smoke?" he asked.

"You know I don't," I replied a bit too sharply. Every time the dove cooed, Geb puffed his cheeks fit to be tied.

"Why don't you build a fire?" I suggested. He knew why.

He asked me if I'd like to see the test reel of an animation of B. Ird. I said I worried I was keeping him from his work. He hurried to set up the projector and the portable silver screen and to pull the blinds. We snapped into darkness in his study; he turned on the beam. The film was still rather crude, a test roll filmed from the tracing papers, not from the plastic cells; so the outlines were sometimes pencil blurred, and it was still black and white. Some light seemed to have bled in, which caused occasional flashes in the frame. But there in rough was a fluid B. Ird Starr. The hero entered from a single vertical slash, stepped out with one foot, enlivening the entire frame by degrees until his beak filled the rectangle and his features disappeared.

This short section was the proposed opening of a pilot series the animator hoped Geb would approve. Geb had written the story, drawn a story board. B. Ird backed against a line that would eventually be a brick wall, and he simply watched the weather change: summer sun angling in the right hand corner, a shedding of leaves that brought fall; winter snow and spring showers all in the blink of an eye. It passed in a little less than a minute. B. Ird's beak moved up to anticipate the precipitation changing from leaves to snow to rain. It followed a leaf to light upon the ground.

Geb opened the blinds. I blinked. "Does he look right?" asked Geb, and I nodded. "They want to change his name; they want ole B. Ird to become Bird Star in this cartoon. After all these years."

"But they're not going to, are they?"

"No," he assured me, then added, "do you know how to calculate the wind chill factor?"

"I've never thought about it."

"You take the wind speed and the temperature," he reached for a table he had made. "Here, see for yourself. It's twenty degrees right now and say the wind is still— what's the wind chill?"

"Twenty," I said. "Let's use the real wind speed."

"I would guess about twenty this morning," said Geb.

"That makes minus nine."

"Let's build a fire, have a cup of tea, then I'll start to work."

Geb opened a cabinet, turned to me and announced, "There's no tea in *here*!" He sounded enthusiastic. Maybe there was tea some other place he had yet to look. And of course I could not help him. I wanted tea, so I smiled and said I really must be going anyway, and that tea was a nice idea but not a necessity. Geb said, "There's coffee. Coffee?"

As I went out the door, Geb hollered, "Bring back some Wagner's when you go to the store."

I had not planned to go shopping, and I had not planned to return. I shouted, "Wagner's?"

"Yeah, Wagner's Wild Bird Seed. It's going to be another cold one tonight. See you later, I've got to work. If Clarice calls, you tell her I'm working away, that she should come back home tomorrow at the latest. It'll all be finished, I'm sure."

After I left, walking patches of dry road between the many patches of ice to my house and thinking all the while of tea for one, Geb called Donald but Donald did not come. He was either asleep or refusing to obey. Geb called, "Donald, Don-ald, DONALD!"

He found Baby Thing on the counterpane just where she had been. She stretched and purred at Geb, who stroked her stomach and talked sweet talk into her ears until she purred so loudly that Donald appeared from under the dust ruffle, shaking his ears. Donald could be quite jealous of Baby Thing, and he always tried to do things that only cats were allowed. Donald attempted the bed, but Geb stopped him, took him by the collar to the door and put him out. Donald saw the whole experience as punishment, an injustice. So he loped out of the yard. Presently, I began to hear a pathetic scratching at the screen door.

"Hello, Donald," I opened the door. Donald replied with a shrug, marching in resolutely with a blast of cold. He planned to stay. "If I had you, I'd call you Kangaroo, maybe Roo for brevity," I told him. "Confidentially, Donald, you could do with a more suitable name." Donald barked as I suspected he might. "Would you like some tea?" He barked once and I put on the kettle.

Meanwhile, Clarice was trying to phone but received a signal of rapid beeps, the signal that my line was somehow interrupted. She hung up and thought she would try again. But she went shopping (there was a very good white sale downtown) and because she returned late, she did not try to phone again.

Geb tried to reach Clarice later on. Of course she was at the sale. He figured he'd guessed wrong. He tried to reach me by phone, but it was out of order, as I already mentioned.

Donald and I had tea and toast. Soon Geb would be walking over to see about Clarice (he was still convinced we were in cahoots) and to discover Donald eating a peanut butter and grape jelly open-faced sandwich as his reward for suffering as he had.

But Donald did not know about the sandwich yet and was slumped beside the hearth, gazing into the fire with poetic indifference toward the cruel world from which he had fled.

Geb glanced into the guest room where Baby Thing slept once again, engaged in the act of dreaming about cat and mouse. Baby Thing often had dreams starring herself. This one began as her dreams did when she dreamed, as she often did, that she was able to read: a cat like Baby Thing, only male, sat down to begin a story book and then became part of the story himself, as herself. The male cat who had begun the book disappeared and Baby Thing followed the red mouse, turned into a cartoon, not a real mouse at all, and Baby Thing, too, turned extravagant and huge, frog gear upon her feet, on her face a mask and snorkel she had once observed Geb use in a swimming pool. Baby Thing would be sure she was dreaming; she would try unsuccessfully to wake.

Her dream would circle; it would go on and on. When she finally woke to take her afternoon food on the square, white typing table upon which all her meals were served, the dream would still be going. Where it went while she was awake, she did not know and did not think about. But when she slept again, the dream would be there, as real as ever. It would begin as it always began, with the disturbing story book she knew by heart. But the old story would twist to surprise her again and again with the old revelation, "Hey, I remember this, I've been here before, and it is I, Baby Thing, who dreams this recurring dream, and it is I who makes this stream swift over remembered white water, remembered rocks and twitches of current. I am dreaming. I am dreaming."

Geb saw Baby Thing's eyes moving under the little lids, but did not know she was dreaming. What she dreamed, he did not know. But it planted an idea in his head concerning B. Ird Starr. Dreaming was a gimmick hard to make work in comics. The dream balloon would take over the square. But he thought he might be able to make it work. Before he opened the study door the phone rang.

"Z—Clarice?"

"I just wanted to tell you—you don't know me—how much I enjoyed Bird Star on the editorial page this morning. I just had to tell you."

"Thanks," said Geb. The editorial page? This guy must really be a nut.

"It's what this country has needed for a long time, a mighty long time," the voice continued. "Someone to speak up for the little people. Washington thinks, if it thinks at all, haw, haw, haw, it thinks it knows everything, but you and I know different—you know, they just *think* they know it all, but you and I see through those Bozos."

Geb said, "Good-bye, now," and hung up.

It's perfect, thought Geb. I'll call the series, "A Dream of the Circus." B. Ird will join the carnival as a freak: a talking bird. What could be more natural—a talking bird, driven by his deformity away from the flock, forced to make a living exhibiting himself. Geb sketched his Ird once lightly before the story began. Ird would take him where he needed to go, he always had.

The new series would make its appearance Easter week; it might win some award of the National Cartoonist Society or drift by unnoticed by all but the hard-core fans. Clarice would return tomorrow, bearing a complete set of Egyptian print sheets, culled from the immense melting pot of the giant white clearance sale of Miller & Rhoads department store, second floor. Baby Thing dreamed her inscrutable mosaics, her distinctive chases, while the mysterious devotee who had telephoned decided to complain by letter to the editor about Geb's rude behavior.

Geb bent his head to the task at hand. Etched with outlines, the paper squares filled with tents and streamers, elephants, midgets, waving flags, cotton candies, magicians, caped clowns and singing lions, swinging trapeze artists, leaping poodles, snow cones, anything Geb had gleaned in numerous childhood visits to the Shriners' circus. But then there were things he was unaware he had ever witnessed that danced onto the drawing board—like bears in tutus—that sparkled in the speech of B. Ird with the grace of a high-wire routine.

The 4:30 train whistled, undetected by the cartoonist at work in the house up the hill. Donald and I kept company by the fire, content until we must rise and make our sandwiches and soup, waiting for Geb to come, unannounced, after the one of us he would miss.

The Strawberry Patch

The grandfather left several things when he passed: a deaf daughter, a retarded son-in-law, farm implements, and a strawberry patch surrounded by spare car parts.

The son-in-law, half-minded as he was, decided to go into business. He decided that he ought to try business of some sort, and since spare parts tended to sparkle in the sun, he began his dealership, specializing in hubcaps. The house radiated hubcaps from top to bottom. Only the red tin roof seemed free of them, although it was not altogether empty, because the son-in-law, several years before the grandfather passed, had begun patching the leaks up there with hubcaps. From a bird's-eye vantage, one could note the gradual distribution of circles amidst the tin slabs. The son-in-law didn't really like using the hubcaps as patch; he liked them nailed onto the planks where he could admire the display. But, so it went, he was forced by poverty to use the materials at hand, and so he did.

The grandfather, when he passed, also left a dog, a dalmatian named Kangaroo who was hated by the son-in-law, but who was very protective of the deaf daughter. She used Kangaroo like a seeing-eye dog, except that she could see wonderfully well. That's clear enough.

The house stood not very far back from a major interstate. It created quite a spectacle, what with all the hubcaps and the Rainbow Bread screen door sagging on its hinges and the hot pink bedsheet curtains at the upstairs windows blowing toward the road all the time. The front porch was half torn off, and cinder blocks starred the steeply sloping front yard. Across the yard, a little to the left, stood a clothesline strung with chenille bedspreads the deaf daughter had made. Occasionally a car would pull off the interstate onto the old road and ramble onto their cracked concrete drive, and someone, usually a woman, would emerge to mull over the daughter's spreads. Once she made one with the portrait of Elvis Presley in its center and it sold like day-old bread. While the customers examined the clothesline goods, the son-in-law often pried loose the hubcaps from their cars. The deaf daughter sold too cheap; he took the balance in metal. It was all fair and square, or so the son-in-law thought.

The grandfather had, from his youth, been considered the grandfatherly type. He brought flowers to the ladies, candies on the least of special occasions, and generally conducted himself in a grandfatherly fashion. Everyone naturally respected him, although he had no actual grandchildren—at least he had none upon his passing. He used to laugh to Victor, his broker, that if he ever did have any they'd probably be deaf *and* dumb, get it? (He didn't like his son-in-law.)

Things continued for some time in much the same manner as before the grandfather's passing. The daughter, Betz, planted the strawberries, watered and hoed and watched them ripen. The son- in-law ran his business in the black by stealing his wares, his own form of capitalism. Kangaroo stayed on merely for the love of Betz. She fed him royally and he brought rabbits and squirrels to the table of the two, who could have starved without them. Two years passed in this way, but something was bound to change.

On a hot afternoon in July, when the son-in-law was up on the roof, a car pulled into the yard and stopped with one of its front tires against a cinder block. The driver got out and opened the back seat; gathering Kangaroo into his arms, he headed toward the screen door. He called out, as loudly as he could, to be heard above the pounding on the roof, but no one came. The driver sweated in the heat. Kangaroo's tongue dripped onto the driver's shirt. Finally the driver lay the dog down on the half of the porch which was there and began to holler. Through the door, he thought he saw someone in the back, so he opened the door and walked straight ahead until he met Betz eating a baloney sandwich. She jumped up as the driver explained about Kangaroo. She tried to read his lips, but he must have been midwestern, because she couldn't follow much. She pointed, instead, to her ears and said, "I can't hear much." The man stopped and motioned her to the porch. It wasn't a bad accident, just a small leg bone snapped, but Kangaroo wouldn't be hunting anymore. The driver gave her one hundred and fifty dollars for a bedspread and disappeared. He was on his way to Ohio with a load of hash.

Betz stretched the one hundred and fifty bucks as far as it would go—into early fall, but after that the food just stopped cold. On a certain Saturday afternoon when the son-in-law came in for lunch he looked at the table and mouthed his question, "Where's it?" Betz sat at the end of the table and shook her head. Thinking that she hadn't understood the question, he repeated, "Where's my lunch?" She shook her head. He stamped his foot and shouted, "My LUNCH, darn it! LUNCH!" She answered him by opening all of the cabinets, finishing with a jerk on the refrigerator. He began to understand, and he began to rub the back of his neck distractedly. Why hadn't she mentioned this at breakfast? He couldn't remember breakfast. For a moment he considered Kangaroo. Kangaroo glared, growling enough. The idea quickly vanished from the son-in-law's mind.

There was nothing. A simple fact. Betz sniffled and

Cathryn Hankla

scrubbed her hands together. She was already starving.But she guessed she'd get better at it. Too bad she'd never succeeded in getting him baptized. Church might come in handy in a few days. Slowly another idea surfaced, and she looked toward the son-in-law, who had lowered his half-existent chin and was pawing the floor with his eyes. "You can get a job!" she declared.

The son-in-law smirked at her, pulled the hair on his ears and checked the refrigerator to see if the light was working. He took it as a sign, went toward the bedroom where he changed his T-shirt and walked out of the yard toward town for the first time in years.

Betz settled in the chair, propped her head on one hand. Kangaroo came up to lick her ankles and make her laugh. It wasn't so bad to be hungry, but Kangaroo was wagging his tail for lunch, too, and that was much harder. Betz rushed into the yard and raked up with her fingers the stale bread crumbs she had scattered for the birds. She covered the bottom of Kangaroo's dish with crumbs and blades of grass she had not been able to help pulling. The dog tried to eat it, getting grass in his whiskers and crumbs under his chin. He lay down to nap without complaining.

Nothing to do but wait until the son-in-law returned. She had too many bedspreads already, left over from the summer. It seemed no one stopped anymore—since the new road had opened and the gas crunch. Only businessmen traveled anymore, and they weren't interested in scenic routes or chenille. Seemed like the only people she saw now were lost, asking for directions back to the new road. And since she didn't know the way, she could hardly have a conversation, even in signs. Sometimes the son-in-law didn't know the way to the access. The people seldom got out of their cars, just rolled down the window and yelled toward the house as if they were at a gas station. The door was open in the summertime, so the son-in-law stumbled out to see if they wanted a spread. He had only sold two the past summer.

While the son-in-law wandered toward town swigging half a Pepsi he found in the ditch, Betz palmed the cool enamel of the kitchen table and placed one cheek against it, closing her eyes against the heat of the day. Kangaroo went immediately to sleep but kept Betz awake with his dream barks and whimpers. She slowly brushed her hands to a cool spot, inching each to an edge as the table warmed beneath her hands. Before she was sure how it happened, one hand opened a small drawer in the side of the table. She felt a seed packet, she thought, lifting it to look—it was half empty, but the remaining seeds jingled like gravel a fish might wrinkle looking for food. She pulled the drawer out and rustled through it to find several half-used seed packets and a scrap of paper written in the grandfather's hand: "Take my advice and make a small garden. Don't use no machines—smell of turned earth, manure, water, light—newspaper, etc."

The son-in-law signed on immediately to run the Ferris wheel and the Rock-N-Roll cages for two weeks starting Saturday. The Amusement Will Travel Corporation had passed him as he walked toward town, given him a lift and a job. The son-in-law didn't know how lucky he was, and he didn't know what he'd eat until next week when he got his first paycheck.

Back in the direction he had come, he walked home, his head light. To pass the time he kicked at a golf ball core which soon proved too fast and too small, so he began to shuffle a stone. It seemed he'd been walking like this for some time, head down to follow the stone, when a slight dusk started falling. Patches of shadow where trees shaded the road blended together as the sun faded. He didn't know how much farther he had to go, and the road didn't look all that familiar now that he noticed it in losing the stone. Behind, faintly, faintly, a whirring, whorring sound bristled against his hearing. Something he couldn't make out, something leaving or coming. In a few seconds he could tell that it was moving toward him, gaining on him and growing louder as he strained to listen. Soon he could hear it clearly even over the noise of his shoes on gravel; he could hear it, but he did not know what it was.

Used to being baffled, a breath away from sprinting quick as a rabbit, the son-in-law held still, he stopped walking and listened. He wanted to turn around and face the sound. Wanting to turn, with something telling him to run for his life, with half a mind he stood stock-still listening to the dull but interesting music, listening to his chest, listening to the prickles of the little hairs at the nape of his neck whispering to face it, *turn*, *turn*.

Pitch black now on the road, the son-in-law walked at a fair clip. His hands hung limp at his sides, tingling, numb, slightly cool. They felt larger, almost webbed through with invisible rubberish skin, or the fur of an animal. He shook them down as if he were a swimmer. A ball of speed, bigger than a star or a planet, stayed just over the mountain until he turned into his yard.

Outside the house he doused his hands in the trough and stomped to feel the earth. Directly he wandered into Betz's newly planted garden, wanting nothing except to plunge his hands into that dirt, and he did, slapping the damp darkness with huge hands. As he worked the dirt like dough, his hands warmed. With fingers laced he cracked his knuckles, beginning to feel again that the hands belonged.

Sun woke Betz first. She smiled, glad to see him beside her and moved quietly from between the sheets. Kangaroo waited in the kitchen, wagging his tail, panting. A green bean hung down from either side of his mouth along with what could have been strands of okra. Patting him, Betz discovered the beans first, then looked through the screen door to the garden patch, overflowing with colors, predominantly green: her pail holds tomatoes, rose and red and orange and yellow until the pail firms, fills, and her feet are webbed with mud the shade of her plaits. She struggles to the back door, sun climbing over the mountain, where the son-in-law roughly rubs light from his eyes, stretches and scratches his back. The tomato harvest at his feet, he blinks, bends, selects, and eats a handsome pink. Kangaroo prefers green beans, but they all have a marvelous breakfast.

While they feast, the son-in-law gets an idea. Soon Betz can hear the hammer pounding nails and the saw slicing two-by-fours easy as bread. The roof, he covers with hubcaps from his collection after sealing it with thick waxy paper. There are bins built for beans and squash and radishes and onions, turnips, all kinds of lettuces and marigolds and sweet williams. The first bin Betz labels is already full of tomatoes. The son-in-law makes a big sign: "FREASH PRODUSE—1 mile" and goes down the highway to flag cars as if he's always known the way.

They never expanded their garden patch. It produced year-round crops of wheat for loaves and loaves of fresh bread, vegetables, some of them colors and shapes the two had no idea what to call, but they sold well all the same. The son-in-law put these in unmarked bins and pretended not to hear when folks asked what they were.

Winter was Betz's favorite season, when she would wake before light, put a log in the stove, and pull on her green rubber boots to go harvest beneath the snow. The orange and cherry and peach and grapefruit and plum and quince and damson trees which now lined the garden, their fruits swollen with color when the world was white, delighted her. By ten o'clock in the morning, the front yard would be jammed with cars, many without hubcaps and many soon to lose them. Nobody complained.

When the time came, their son sprouted bright as a pumpkin, always humming as he helped his mother hoe. A natural with anything that grew, he was fated to win the 4-H competition with geraniums and goats. Without a doubt, he inherited his grandfather's strawberry patch.

In Search of Literary Heroes

The Mother, it seemed, could read through anything. She read through the Harvard Classics, mysteries, romances, detective fictions, best sellers, biographies, cookbooks, partially condensed, digested novels by the scores. When she was a little girl it had been her recreation, having many older sisters to do the chores, to go to the library, biweekly, in the summertime, and struggle home with tall, two armfuls of books. Then, it had been her pleasure to sit, on an open porch at the front of the three-story white house, and dangle her feet while she read.

The Mother, it has been said, could and did read through anything. Once, and this is true, she read through an earthquake. Of course no one knew it was an earthquake, we believed it was the powder plant simply exploding one more time, and we saw the boasting sign turn back the number of hours of safe work, in our minds. But it was an earthquake which made the china cups quiver in the hutch. Two Santa plates, out of season, tried to break by running along the indention where they sat. But they didn't succeed. The Mother looked up from her book and asked, "Couldn't you be quieter in there?" The daughter was with a friend, in her blue room, playing the records of aging Rock Stars when the needle staggered across her favorite song, "Bird on the Wire."

The Mother read through anything. She held the book up to her face when she was younger, but farther from her face when she grew older. Around the edges of the open book, her hair grew shorter and lighter as years passed. She got glasses and her arms read more comfortably. When the father lost his job, she finished the chapter. When the daughter scraped her head on a rock, which had pelted her from an open sky, the Mother had to stop in the middle of a sentence. She was often the dummy at Bridge in order to read through the tricks.

Seasons may come and go, children, presidents, and with them the significant change in the Mother was to shift from chair in the living room by the window to chaise longue in the sun. No, the sun would not bother her. She had the best tan, which faded the slowest of all the tans of all the mothers. It even outlasted the bikini-mothers' tans. She came in when the sun sank, fixed supper, washed dishes, and picked up the book. When the daughter called the Mother to tell her that her book had been accepted by a publisher, the Mother had to leave a better one to answer the phone.

Here's a short list of things the Mother did or could not read through: childbirth (she was unconscious), driving (it made her dizzy), church (never), Christmas Eve, Perry Mason, weddings (these, she cried through), golf, burials, gardening, sleep, and she did not read through all of Joyce Carol Oates.

It was only natural that the daughter learned to read before she was born. It was, perhaps, not as natural as it might have been, that the daughter came to write books. Books were not to be bought or owned, books were something you read. You borrowed them, you read them, and you passed them on or returned them. You did not write your name in them. You did not keep them. The idea of possessing books was quite beside the Mother. Other people bought books they didn't read, other people liked to look at books, or touch them, hold them, show them, talk about them, argue with them, but the Mother merely read them. And often the Great Pyrenees scratched at the bottom of her bowl or lumbered through rooms while the Mother read.

To record the facts is never to boast. To boast about the facts is simply boring, and, for the record, the facts may boast of the absurd. This is surely the case with the Mother, who, once upon a glorious time, anytime at all, began to read the latest Dick Francis novel at the crack of dawn. It was an ordinary dawn promising an ordinary day, and it was begun in an ordinary way. If the book, however, had contained anything of the ordinary the Mother wouldn't have wasted her sight. When she had read through the first three chapters, the sun failed and a slight storm brewed up to drown the greensward with healthy April puddles. Forsythia dropped the rest of its blossoms, the weeping cherry did the same. The world was changed, but not so the Mother. She rose, showered, then breakfasted on chapter five, after packing the father a brown-bag lunch. The daughter was at school or perhaps not yet born. Or perhaps it would be a childless marriage after all, who knew, who cared? For certainly, it would not last without fiction.

Skeleton

There was madness in the family. The grandmother knew. (Her sister had hanged herself when it was reported what the Nazis had been doing to the Jews.) The grandfather knew. (His brothers yelled at their wives and deafened their children.) The mother understood. (Her husband was a problem all to himself—he had gone to the funeral of his aunt without a clue. He'd imagined she'd smoked herself to death. He never knew until he was so old that everyone assumed he did know, and the truth slipped out between dinner and dessert one Sunday afternoon at his mother's table.)

"Now you've done it!" his brother snapped.

"Oh no!" his sister covered her mouth so recently stuffed with potato that it ached. "I thought he knew."

"And of course you're correct," answered the brother. "Because now he does."

But Gerald handled it very well, as far as anyone knew. He just said, "Oh, I never knew," and went about stirring butter into the mound of mashed potato on his plate. He added pepper and salt while his brother and sister lambasted each other.

"You've spoiled Mother's dinner," the grandmother remarked sadly. Everyone, except the grandchildren and Gerald, turned guiltily toward her. Gerald had emerged blameless once again. He finished with two slices of pie—rhubarb and strawberry and apple a la mode. He poured his coffee into his saucer, lapped it like a cat, and had another steaming cup while his sister and brother declined dessert but remained at the table to stew. Gerald always knew how to please his mother, who knew how to bake an excellent apple pie. His brother and sister made their children remain seated until Gerald had finished, but Gerald's wife, Candy, let their two children leave to play outside as soon as they were through.

As a result of knowing what good manners were, Bruce's and Mildred's children were quietly malignant, while Gerald's were noisily innocent of any resentment toward animals, vegetables, or adults. Gin and Johnny even enjoyed cooked spinach. So the grandmother had developed a soft spot for them, too, and everyone instantly knew it. But being the favorites brought its own brand of grief as well as its reward.

But why was Gerald so different? He had been born during a quarter moon at the end of summer, right on time. Little Lord Fauntleroy's velvet had not been foreign to him, growing up, being photographed each birthday in a slightly altered version of last year's suit until a new suit was constructed, and, at last, Lord Fauntleroy went out of style. His mother, undaunted, learned to sew. You might presume from all of this that Gerald was either the oldest child or the youngest. This is not true. He existed in the middle, between a brother who excelled at baseball and a sister who excelled at crewel and bowling. The only athletic event Gerald ever enjoyed was rolling down the little slope in the back yard. Later, he could be seen riding a bicycle, delivering newspapers, but his childhood was spent, in the main, rolling down the hill.

It is not surprising that he developed a distorted sense of reality. Long after he learned to ride the bike he sometimes had great spills because he was prone to looking at the world from upside down. The urge would bowl him over, out of the blue, so to speak, and he would turn his head on end and study the sky. When walking he simply stopped and stood on his head or put his head between his legs for a spell. But when riding a bicycle, the unorthodox behavior left him in a sprawl. Luckily, he lived in a small town and no car had ever come just at the moment he turned his hands underneath the bars to gaze precariously up. He could ride for a block or more like this before a stray rock or pothole unhinged his grip. One fall, the first day of school, he wrote the obligatory composition about how he had spent his summer vacation—recovering from a broken leg. No one but his mother had known until the newspaper published the essay as an example of excellent seventh-grade prose exactly how the accident occurred. The head carrier released him that same afternoon. Gerald decided to become a writer.

This was his first poem, scribbled at the bottom of his math homework:

The sky is bold
It broke my toe—
I have been told
That I should know—
Better

He instinctively adopted the dashes of Dickinson.

When Gerald saw his composition in the newspaper he read and reread it, paying particular attention to the way his name looked at the bottom of the several paragraphs. One of the oddest things in life, he concluded, is to see one's name in print, or written in someone else's hand. He couldn't say why this affected him so strongly. He tried, as a result, to change the way he wrote his name. He tried so many different pens that his mother finally had a fit, "I insist that you stop this instant!" "Stop what?" Gerald inquired, amazed at her rage as he scribbled the back of an envelope with variations of his name, pens spread around him in a circle of color. "Stop writing your name—and just look at all those pens! Where did you find them all?" "I bought them with my lunch money," he confessed. And he was forbidden to "collect" another pen until every one of these ran out of ink. Then, he was only allowed to buy refills. Gerald looked, as quickly as possible, for another job.

After losing a job, it is harder to find one. However, his early publication had brought him name recognition, at the grocery store. No one read books, Gerald discovered, but everyone read the newspaper—even those who proudly claimed not to waste time reading. Local news didn't count, at least didn't stigmatize one as an "egg-head." Gerald was one notch above these readers, so he was hired by the manager after telling his name, even though he had been told that no help was needed. He became a bagger. He wore a necktie to work that didn't clip on; he smiled and told his customers, mainly mothers of his school friends, to "come back" and they always did, on a regular basis. Gerald was so good at his job that he was promoted to cashier; he rose rapidly because he turned down tips. This impressed the manager with his honesty and confirmed his hiring as a wise decision. The manager went up, too—becoming a district manager. Gerald went up with him—becoming the store assistant manager at the age of seventeen. A marvel. All because of having broken his leg in a literary fashion; all because he had written and been published. For years he tried to repeat his success without success. In fact, he found that his early publication caused teachers to think that he thought that he knew it all. They seemed determined to punish him. George Stein got the editorship of "The Cougar's Tale," not Gerald. And because he had gotten the job in the grocery store, he hardly had any time to write. When he heard the definition of "cosmic irony" in English class, Gerald merely signed his name into his notebook. He looked toward college as if it promised the only exit from a house of mirrors. He didn't care that his father chose the school and wouldn't let him apply anywhere else. Like most of the other freshmen, he arrived at college determined to shed his old skin, to make new friends, to be himself, and to get away from himself at the first opportunity.

The prospect of a year of proverbial "English and Composition" did not bother Gerald. On the contrary, it presented itself as a grand opportunity. The first assignment was to describe a room. Having chosen the room, he went about taking notes, unaware that the classroom buildings were locked at six o'clock. The next morning he emerged from his English classroom with vast hunger pains and a finished essay he had only to type. In several days the essays were handed back—everyone's except Gerald's, which was read to the class by the professor, then placed into Gerald's blushing, perspiring fingers as if it had been unearthed at Pompeii. Gerald, ecstatic, had become a despised hero once again. But late that evening a girl introduced herself and asked for help on the upcoming paper. The assignment was to describe a process. His first girlfriend; he had no choice but to go steady before the first year was out, and, upon graduation, to marry her and have two children, a boy and a girl.

Gerald went back to the grocery store, as manager, and wrote novels on weekends. He had written four novels in six years but had yet to find a publisher or to properly "organize his audience" when he was promoted to district manager upon the retirement of his old benefactor, Mr. Lynch. He took the promotion and the raise because he was promised three-day weekends two times a month. He told people that his hobby was roses until, when he was forty-eight, the following story appeared in *The Saturday Evening Post*.

THE ROSE GARDEN
(A story by Gerald Sackett)

When I was small, my aunt Virginia would take me by the hand and lead me, dressed up like a princess for the visit, into her rose garden. One Saturday, near the end of the war, she stopped, with me in tow, before a pale yellow bud and remarked that my dress matched the rose. This was her highest compliment, and I thanked my mother in my heart for having insisted upon the yellow dress when I had asked for a blue one. Then, as always, I followed Aunt Virginia from bush to bush as she told me a story held together by roses.

"There was a little girl who woke each night to the sound of the coal train's whistle. When the whistle disturbed her sleep she'd hear her parents' voices raised, in an argument, coming up the stairwell. She'd have to plunge her head into her pillow, folding its sides up and anchoring them with her arms to go back to sleep."

"Why were her parents fighting?" I interrupted.

"They didn't have any money," Aunt Virginia answered. "See that rose there? It's called Summer Sunshine."

"What was the little girl's name?"

"Her name was Rose. Rose was very poor; she didn't have pretty summer frocks like you do, and her parents didn't have time to tend flowers like these. Do you know that one, there?"

It had deep red petals. I could smell its fragrance, although the blossom rose taller than my head. "Mister..." I said.

"Yes, Mister Lincoln!" She was as happy as if I had gotten it right. "Do you know who Lincoln was?"

"He was President."

"Yes, and always remember that he freed the slaves." I nodded my head, afraid she had forgotten about Rose, the saddest girl I'd ever imagined. "Where does Rose live?" I asked.

"In Virginia."

"How old was she?" I asked.

"She was your age. Do you know this deep pink?" I shook my head. "It's Southern Belle." She snipped the stem expertly and told me to carry it near the bloom so the thorns wouldn't prick.

"One morning when Rose woke, she went downstairs to the kitchen, but her mother wasn't fixing any breakfast. Instead of her mother, she found a note scotchtaped to the refrigerator.

> *Dear Sweetheart,*
> *I have to go away for a little while, because your father and I don't get along anymore. Daddy will take care of you until I can find a job. Be a good girl and don't make Daddy mad.*
>
> > *Love,*
> > *Mother*

"Rose fixed herself some cereal without spilling the

milk. Her daddy had left for work. Before leaving for
school, Rose folded the note and put it in the back of
her arithmetic book, where the answers were.

"In school that day Rose's teacher told the class about
a tower in Paris, France, that was 984 feet high. Do
you know the name of the tower?" She paused. "Eiffel,
just like the rose." Aunt Virginia snipped a light pink,
overstuffed like a pillow with the feathers pouching out,
and handed it to me. She cut one that had yet to open
that already looked like a blossom it was so long. Aunt
Virginia laid my roses in a basket looped over her arm
when I was tired of carrying one in each hand.

"Where did Rose's mother go?"

"She went to France."

"Why?"

"Because she had to get away."

"Did she come back?"

"She tried to, but she couldn't because of the war.
They wouldn't let anyone but the soldiers leave. She
wrote Rose a letter every day, but Rose's father kept the
letters from her so she'd forget about her mother."

"Did she?"

"No. She never forgot. And when she was grown up,
she went to France to find her mother." Aunt Virginia
stopped to cut one more rose with a lemon sherbet bloom
so large I held it in both hands. I knew its name, but I
couldn't remember it. Each petal was touched pink around
the edges.

"I know its name," I whispered.

"Good," said Aunt Virginia; she trusted me.

We went inside and ate big slices of chocolate cake
and drank tall, icy glasses of milk at the mahogany table,
polished and shiny as the china plates. It was the realest
story I'd ever been told. Our roses filled a purple vase
at the center of the table, reflecting from the dark wood,
muted pink and yellow, muted pink and red.

The next Saturday I stood between my parents, each of
my hands swallowed by one of theirs, beneath the striped

canopy of the funeral company. It was a sunny day with a little wind flapping under the ruffled canvas. When I learned, years later, that Aunt Virginia had hanged herself in the two-story stairwell of her house, I remembered the blanket of roses on her casket, pink and yellow, yellow, pink and red: Mr. Lincoln and Summer Sunshine, Southern Belle, Eiffel Tower, King's Ransom, and Peace.

If it were Dark

If it were dark for long enough; if we were left in darkness not minutes but for years at a time, crowded into darkness as if into the vast hold of a ship which was bound never to land; if it were dark without a hope, however distant, of escape or of the least bit of an indulgence in light: how long would it take before we touched the people to our left and right? Before we greeted them? How long until we descended again into isolation, unable to bear breathing the same air as the others? If then the light, forgotten, inappropriately clicked on, would we wander, blinking and blind, away from our fellow captives? Or, would we be loyal to them?

These are the kinds of things I think about—the time passes as I weigh one thought, one alternative against another. Either/or; either/or. My dad always called me "The Diplomat of the Family," or "The Lucky One." I guess he needed somebody to be lucky.

There are people here who wish they had died or would die, some who try to hasten the process. But I'm lucky to be alive; and I never really felt that way until now.

One time I wrote a story about a girl who hated school. I had a lot in common with the girl, except for the main conflict. It kind of made me feel creepy when my teacher couldn't tell the difference between the girl in the story and me. Why would I be showing him the story if I hated school? Cary ate a big piece of chocolate cake for breakfast whenever she could get it and tried to get her boyfriend to say he really liked Cary's best friend, not Cary. Why would a real person do anything that ridiculous? I never showed him another story, because whenever I thought about what he might say a terrible thought occurred to me—that I could make Mr. Mahn think I was a shoplifter or an anorexic or even obsessed with refrigerators if I wrote a story about someone who was. It occurred to me that I might convince Mr. Mahn that I was in love with him if I wrote a story about a girl infatuated with her teacher. Could I convince Mr. Mahn that he was in love with me? The worst consequence of this temptation was that it would wash through me at the oddest moments. In Mr. MacCarthy's biology lab, in the middle of dissecting a frog with my partner, Susie Parks, I couldn't stop laughing. We found the heart of the frog and I touched it with the end of my pencil. I kept thinking how I would write a story in which a tenth grader dissected an earthworm while her teacher wrote her a love letter on school stationery. I still don't know why it had to be school stationery. Mr. MacCarthy thought I was hysterical because of the frog and sent me to the nurse to lie down until the end of the period. He decided that I was "sensitive." Mr. Mahn had told him about my story. Mr. MacCarthy might have read the story for all I know—lots of things went on in the teachers' lounge you never heard about, but you felt the nuances. If teachers began being "concerned" about a particular student you could bet it was happening because of some remark made in the lounge. But after a few days they would forget about all the problems you were supposedly having and start hassling you for homework like everyone else.

If we dream of things, are we then thinking of the things that really matter to us, or are we then indulging in things we don't have leisure to experience at any other time? Are dreams like a vacation or like going to work?

I dream all the time, and I still don't know the answer to these questions. Last night, for instance, I dreamed I met myself twice in the same dream. First I was introduced to a short, dark girl who shook my hand and said her name, Lois Lessing. It was my name too. Later on I visited a tall woman in a hospital. I knew she had had a double mastectomy and some plastic surgery on her face, which was smooth as an ironed sheet. She shook my hand, introducing herself, "I'm Lois Lessing." I said that was weird and told her my name was Lois Lessing too. It turned out that the tall Lois Lessing had been a Nazi sympathizer. If she had cancer now, she deserved it. I didn't find out anything about the first Lois. When I woke up I couldn't stop wondering why I was so sure my name was Lois in the dream when it wasn't really.

I had the worst nightmare I've ever had when I was about five. It took place in my usual neighborhood. I rode my bike, as always. My whole family assembled on a neighbor's steps in the distance. I pumped the bike as hard as I could, so I wouldn't miss my uncles and aunts, my parents, cousins, my sister and brother. Even the cat, Big Orange, was there on the step. Just as I jumped from my bike to rush toward them they all rose and began ripping their faces off like Halloween masks. Underneath the masks were dark, formless features, razor teeth, and slimy eye-sockets. I noticed that their hands were more like claws. In close-ups, each one peeled off his smiling face and started toward me as the creature he had become. I tried to run, to pick up my bike and ride away from them, but I stood as each mask fell to the ground, my heart pumping like an overburdened steam engine as the figures circled me, their prey. Mr. Mahn would probably think anyone who had a dream like that must hate his family. It can't be that logical, though.

They say that since I can't talk about what happened to me I should write it, that if I once write it I'll be okay. I tell them that I haven't written about anything else since the first day they handed me the notebook, but they're not satisfied.

They want me to date each entry I make, as if I were measuring each day by what I say or don't say. I mark off the days on the calendar but I don't date my words. They're timeless, that's what's good about them. I remember things, make up things, think out things, it's all the same. It's not linear, and that bothers them. I used to like swimming underwater better than on top—

Lambcake

It was her birthday and she knew it. She liked the fact of being newly old and nearly young no longer. Her mother had laid her smocked dress on the pink ballerina chair the night before and told her to be sure to fasten all the buttons.

"If you can't reach them at the back of the neck, I'll do it. Just call me in the morning."

The sun pounded into the room with the timbre of a kettledrum, at six. Usually she would sleep until nine or ten on Saturdays, but not today. She brushed her sleepy hair, pulled on her socks, and buttoned up her dress. The party wasn't until the afternoon, two o'clock her mother had said.

"Will they bring presents?" she had asked.

"Yes, but you must behave as if each gift were your favorite."

This seemed the most impossible task ever assigned to her. Billy would give her something dumb for sure. He was only invited because his mother was in the Bridge Club. She already knew she'd like Tisha's present best. Tish had almost told her what it was three times last week while they were marching in twos to the lunch room for "baloney hats." During the multiplication test Tish had nearly flunked because she kept wanting to tap out her secret in code: one tap = A; two taps, B, and so forth. Tish couldn't do the elevens anyway—that's probably why her attention turned to other things.

At six the world looked like a frozen popsicle, the yard speckled with frosty shadows, the sky as dark as the inside of a dream. She'd had a real bad dream once: all the people in her family had ripped off their faces to reveal monster faces beneath. The other scary dream

Cathryn Hankla

she remembered was of a little man—maybe a Mexican, like the Frito Bandito—who jumped through her bedroom window and tickled her awake. At first it was funny, but then he jumped back into her room faster and faster, tickling her harder and harder until she knew he was trying to kill her in the only way he could. A third bad dream was of King Kong. Her bedroom was on the second floor; the night after she'd seen *King Kong* for the first time, he had put his face against her window and looked in on her while she slept.

I wish they'd quit taking my pages away as I write them. I'd like to look back sometimes and finish things up. I never finished what I started yesterday about the birthday party. I never got to the cake, which would have explained the title. I'm sure I never got that far. I'd like to hide these pages, but they disappear when I go to the shower or to the dining room or the television room in the evening. Then I have to start all over. I'm going to ask Sherry about it tomorrow.

Sherry says I'll get the pages back, but I don't think so. Not one has come back yet. I feel like stopping altogether, but I told Sherry that and she suggested it was a rotten idea. I get the feeling that I'll really be in for it if I stop writing. I might never go home, or something. If I keep writing I might go home again, and then I'll get all the pages back, when I leave. It's better than watching television with all the others. All I have to say is that I'm going back to my room to write and they smile and let me go. The only problem is that then I really have to come up with something. The day I stop, I'm not sure what would happen. Before they gave me the notebook it was worse.

Janey woke up. She looked around the apartment for her

clothes. She headed for the elevator. No one was in the apartment with her. No one was in the elevator, either. She didn't have a coat to wear out into the snow, but she had cowboy boots with imitation fur lining. Patrick had given them to her the day before he split for Arizona.

"Wide open spaces," he'd grinned.

"Like the corners of your mind," she'd replied.

Walking out into the blowing snow, Janey felt like the little match girl, but she had nothing to sell.

Went to the bathroom and saw blood. I flushed it fast so they wouldn't know, but it's scary all the same. I don't feel like writing today. If I stand on my chair I can see the interstate in the distance. I bet those big trucks with "Grace" on the side are out there. If I could get into one of those I could go far.

Today they came and took my temperature and brought me breakfast in bed. It's nicer than going to the dining hall. I ate everything on the plate except the sugar packages for the coffee. The plastic utensil they brought is called a spork. Spork and beans for lunch, and a hotdog. The food tastes better in bed than any food I've ever had. They give me big pills every four hours. They take my temperature then too and my blood pressure, which is normal. Ice cream for dessert. I didn't go to the showers today.

*   *   *

They didn't take what I wrote yesterday! It's here. I wish I had that story back now. I'm still in bed, taking the pills and eating off a tray. Today the food doesn't taste good, but it's okay. I asked them what was wrong with me but they didn't say. I wish I felt more like starting another story; this time I might be able to finish it. I can try it, anyway.

Cathryn Hankla

JANEY'S LIFE STORY

Janey's father had been a drugstore cowboy, who never married her mother. Her mother never told her he was dead or anything like that. She married someone else right away, so Janey always had two fathers, Gary and Irby, her real father. She hardly ever saw her real father; and her mother referred to Gary as "your dad," and to Irby as Irby. Janey thought of her real father on a first-name basis and naturally called Gary "Dad." It wasn't confusing at all until Janey went to college and reflected on her family. It really didn't make sense to her, after that. She hated going home for holidays then, because she didn't feel natural anymore, and it showed. Her mother asked at Thanksgiving if she hated them. Janey tried every excuse she could think of for not going home for Christmas; nothing worked, nothing happened until Patrick came along the fall of her sophomore year. Then it all changed. She and Patrick were together night and day and they didn't care who knew it.

She didn't know if Patrick had had other girlfriends—they didn't talk about his past. Sometimes Janey would ask him something and he would reply, "That's the past." She got the feeling that it was less that he wanted to forget it or that he had forgotten it than that it was enshrined, and he didn't want her to know about it. She told him anything he asked. She was afraid that if she didn't answer his questions, he'd leave her, and she was afraid she was falling in love with him. She wanted him to stay around long enough for her to find out.

One thing he asked her right away was if she'd sleep with him. She said she'd think about it.

"You'll sleep on it?" he asked.

"Yeah, maybe I'll let you know tomorrow."

The next night they had spent at Patrick's apartment. His roommates were away for the weekend. Later, Janey wondered who he would have asked instead if he hadn't asked her, and if he would have asked someone else right away. Probably, she thought. But then, she didn't know for sure. Patrick was someone who'd managed to keep his mystery. He managed it by leaving questions unanswered; Janey figured it was easier for a man to do that. But then women, no matter how many questions they answered, could still keep theirs if they wanted. Maybe it was because men never asked them the questions which would end the mystery. They knew better; at least Patrick did. He didn't ask her if she'd slept with anyone before. She figured he thought she had or she wouldn't have slept with him.

Back to a blank slate. I must have fallen asleep, or they just remembered. I feel like my mind is being wiped with an eraser. It's no use writing anything real anymore. I need to keep all the real things inside so I can go back over them, turn them over in my mind. If I write them down they'll be lost.

Janey felt as if she were dying from a brain tumor—her head pounded whenever she lifted it from the pillow. Her legs, numb and aching, lay uncovered for hours without her knowing to cover them. A nurse finally checked on her, bringing a tray of lunch and tucking the blankets beneath her feet.

"How are we feeling this afternoon?" she asked.

Janey tried to mouth a response.

"How are we feeling?" the nurse repeated, arranging the tray across the bed like a strap.

"My head hurts," Janey mumbled.

"Oh, it does?"

"Yeah."

"I'd better take a look at the chart—see if you can have a sedative after lunch."

Janey looked at the tray—mashed potatoes and baked chicken, jello, roll, milk, hot tea. She raised the thermal cup to her lips and blew across the brown water before sipping in a breath of tea. When she swallowed, after holding it in her mouth for several seconds, she felt the liquid moving down her throat, thought she felt it hit the empty lining of her stomach, thought she felt the pores of her face steaming awake with the cup so near. She couldn't remember for a moment why she was here. She should have walked out yesterday, afterward. Complications. Observation.

Patrick would be in to visit her soon. The flowers he'd left waved on the table beside the phone. She hoped her mother didn't try to get in touch—there was no reason why she should, but you never knew. Mothers were psychic, Janey believed. She believed hers was. Her roommate couldn't tell her anything, but that was just the problem. Janey's mother was the type to automatically call the police before checking at Patrick's apartment. Then she'd start on the hospitals, in alphabetical order. Janey had to get out of the hospital before the evening. When the nurse returned, smiling, with the pain killer clenched within a plastic cup, Janey refused it and tried to chew some chicken. Before the nurse squeaked out Janey was throwing up. She asked for another cup of tea, lay back on her pillows and waited. Her doctor, whom she'd never seen, would be in soon, the nurse assured. Janey told her she had to get home.

"We're worried about you, Polly," Sherry said. "There's no reason for you to stay in bed all day. You can go back to your old schedule anytime you're ready. It's not good to be isolated from the others, you know. They miss you. Gerald's been asking about you every meal; he's saving your place. Are you listening, Polly?"

Sherry left soon afterward. She said she'd come back and visit Polly tomorrow. Sherry looked at the notebook but didn't ask about it for once. Polly felt relieved. I thought for sure Sherry would take the notebook with her. I wanted to ask about the missing pages, but Polly didn't want to know.

If it were Dark   79

Janey woke after what seemed like days. It was dark outside, beyond the circle of light enclosing the hospital parking lot like a cage. Patrick was looking at her from a chair in the corner of the room, with his hat dangling from one hand.

"Are you okay?" he asked.

"Yeah," she said.

"I missed my Spanish exam," he said. "But I would have failed anyway, so no problem."

"I'm sorry," Janey said.

"When are you coming home?"

"I don't know—tomorrow, I think."

"Your mother called."

"Oh brother," Janey sighed. "What'd she want?"

"She took it fine."

"What did you tell her?"

"The truth."

"Don't be funny."

"I'm not."

"You told her the truth!" Janey tried to sit up but only managed to prop on an elbow. When Patrick perched on the bed like a penguin, Janey lay back on the pillows, surrendering.

"What should I have told her? She thought you'd died or something. She was relieved, I think, when I told her."

"Is she coming?"

"Tomorrow morning," Patrick said. "I've got my history exam at nine, a chance for a B if I don't blow it."

"Hello, Polly," Sherry pulled open the curtains and yanked the blind cord down. "It's a beautiful, sunny day!"

Polly blinked; the bright sun made her eyes water. It was in the dark that she belonged.

"What's wrong, Polly?" asked Sherry. Polly put her pillow over her face, turned and faced the wall, hugging the covers to her neck, holding them in her fists.

· Cathryn Hankla

"Polly, you can tell me, it's Sherry. Polly, can you hear me?"

Polly nodded, she was afraid not to. Sherry might call the others.

"Good," said Sherry. "Now take the pillow off; now do what I say: let go of the covers and turn this way. Good. Now take the pillow off your head. Take down the pillow, and look at me . . . Polly, why not take that ugly pillow down?"

"You didn't say 'Simon says,'" said Polly.

"This is not a game. This is *real*, Polly, real life, and I'm asking you to please take the pillow off your face and look at me so we can talk."

I wanted Polly to keep the pillow over her face, but she took it off. I don't know why she had to do what Sherry said.

* * *

"The doctor said you've got to take it easy for a while. You lost a lot of blood during the... operation," Janey's mother turned her head toward the closet and began stuffing things into the flight bag Janey had borrowed.

"I have to finish exams."

"No, I've talked to the dean and you've got incompletes in everything until after the holidays. You're coming back with me."

"I need to go by Patrick's first."

"Good morning," said Sherry. "Your mother's in the lobby; she's come to visit you."

"You didn't tell me she was coming today," I said.

"Yes, I did. I told you yesterday. Do you want to see her?"

"No," said Polly.

"Why not?" Sherry asked.

"I really want to see her," I said. "But she's mad at me, so I'd rather not."

"She's not mad at you."

"How do you know?" asked Polly.

"She loves you very much, and she's come a long way on the train just to see how you are. She has to go back to work tomorrow. She got off from work just to see you for an hour. She looks dressed up, and she's had her hair done. Don't you want to see her?" Sherry asked.

"Yeah."

"Listen, I'll call you in a few days, before I leave for Christmas."

"Are you coming to visit?" Janey asked.

"I'm planning a little trip. Need to get out by myself for a week or so, so I guess I won't see you until next semester."

"Oh."

"Don't worry, Janey. I'm just going out to Arizona to see Bill."

"Bill?"

"The past," Patrick answered. They kissed good-bye as Janey's mother looked out the window.

"How was the visit with your mother?" asked Sherry.

"You should know," said Polly.

"How?"

"You read the notebook on the subject," said Polly.

"You didn't say much about it," Sherry said. "You wrote more about Janey than about yourself. Why was that, Polly?"

"I don't know," said Polly.

"Is Janey you?" Sherry asked. "Who is Janey?"

"Janey is my character," said Polly.

"Oh, I see," Sherry said. "Your mother said she thought you were ready to go home. What do you think?"

"It's not up to me," I said.

"Yes it is."

At that hour of the night the "Wishy Wash" was an all night cafe. You couldn't tell the students from the derelicts in its equivocal light, but you could be pretty sure the big women with swinging behinds weren't students, never had been. Their children slept on the turquoise plastic seats which only a child could be comfortable in. Young men nursed styrofoam cups of coffee or chocolate laced with rum; old men did the same, the broken veins in their noses glowing red above the steaming cups. Dryer bells dinged, people rose to meet them; spin cycles clicked into place and no one moved. Folding his shirts in the corner, on the cracked formica which was looking more like its marble model each day, was Patrick. He turned to the brunette, who gazed into a dryer a few feet away, and asked,

"Do you need any soap? I've got some left."

"No," she answered. "I've finished washing. Wish the dryer would stop, but it's got five more minutes."

"I'll wait for you," he said, almost absently. "We could go for a beer."

"I don't drink."

"Or back to my place."

"It doesn't have to be either/or," she said, without looking from the window of the dryer. "We could do something else, or we could do nothing."

It was several days before Janey really looked at him, by daylight. In the dark it was amazing how much his face felt like her own. She didn't care if she ever saw him again.

"Are you ready to go?" Sherry asked.

"Yes," I said, handing her the notebook. There weren't many pages left, but I thought she ought to have it.

"It's yours." She handed me a folder of loose pages.

"You're really giving them back?"

"Really. I said I'd give them back, didn't I?" I could tell she was a little hurt that I hadn't believed her before.

"I just didn't think they'd let you. Did they keep a copy?"

"No. Neither did I."

"Did you like Janey's Life Story?" I asked.

"Not as much as Polly's, or yours."

We laughed.